The
Christmas Stories

Charles Dickens

The
Christmas Stories

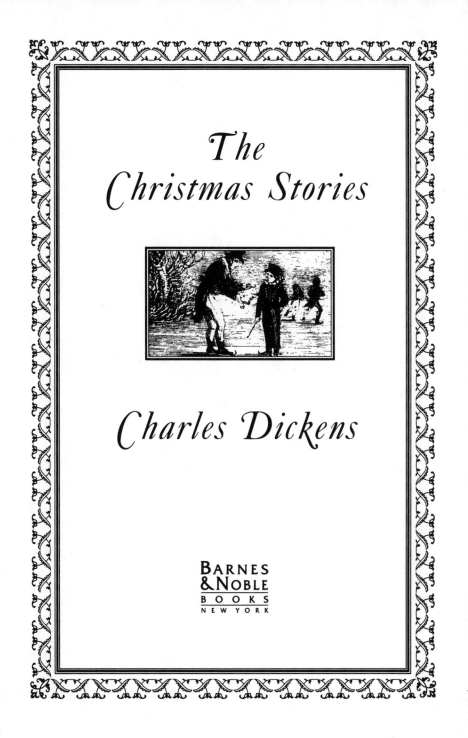

Charles Dickens

**BARNES
&NOBLE
BOOKS**
NEW YORK

This edition published by Barnes & Noble, Inc.

1994 Barnes & Noble Books

Slipcase Set ISBN 1-56619-447-4

Volume ISBN 1-56619-486-5

Book design by James Sarfati

Printed and bound in the United States of America

M 9 8 7 6 5 4 3 2

CONTENTS

A Christmas Tree

 have been looking on, this evening, at a merry company of children assembled round that pretty German toy, a Christmas Tree. The tree was planted in the middle of a great round table, and towered high above their heads. It was brilliantly lighted by a multitude of little tapers; and everywhere sparkled and glittered with bright objects. There were rosy-cheeked dolls, hiding behind the green leaves; and there were real watches (with movable hands, at least, and an endless capacity of being wound up) dangling from innumerable twigs; there were French-polished tables, chairs, bedsteads, wardrobes, eight-day clocks, and various other articles of domestic furniture (wonderfully made, in tin, at Wolverhampton), perched among the boughs, as if in preparation for some fairy housekeeping; there were jolly, broad-faced little men, much more agreeable in appearance than many real men—and no wonder, for their heads took off, and showed them to be full of sugar-plums; there

were fiddles and drums; there were tambourines, books, work-boxes, paint-boxes, sweetmeat-boxes, peep-show boxes, and all kinds of boxes; there were trinkets for the elder girls, far brighter than any grown-up gold and jewels; there were baskets and pincushions in all devices; there were guns, swords, and banners; there were witches standing in enchanted rings of pasteboard, to tell fortunes; there were teetotums, humming-tops, needle-cases, pen-wipers, smelling-bottles, conversation-cards, bouquet-holders; real fruit, made artificially dazzling with gold leaf; imitation apples, pears, and walnuts, crammed with surprises; in short, as a pretty child, before me, delightedly whispered to another pretty child, her bosom friend, "There was everything, and more." This motley collection of odd objects, clustering on the tree like magic fruit, and flashing back the bright looks directed towards it from every side —some of the diamond-eyes admiring it were hardly on a level with the table, and a few were languishing in timid wonder on the bosoms of pretty mothers, aunts, and nurses—made a lively realization of the fancies of childhood; and set me thinking how all the trees that grow and all the things that come into existence on the earth, have their wild adornments at that well-remembered time.

Being now at home again, and alone, the only person in the house awake, my thoughts are drawn back, by a fascination which I do not care to resist, to my own childhood. I begin to consider, what do we all remember best upon the branches of the Christmas Tree of our own young Christmas days, by which we climbed to real life.

Straight, in the middle of the room, cramped in the

freedom of its growth by no encircling walls or soon-reached ceiling, a shadowy tree arises; and, looking up into the dreamy brightness of its top—for I observe in this tree the singular property that it appears to grow downward towards the earth—I look into my youngest Christmas recollections!

All toys at first, I find. Up yonder, among the green holly and red berries, is the Tumbler with his hands in his pockets, who wouldn't lie down, but whenever he was put upon the floor, persisted in rolling his fat body about, until he rolled himself still, and brought those lobster eyes of his to bear upon me—when I affected to laugh very much, but in my heart of hearts was extremely doubtful of him. Close beside him is that infernal snuff-box, out of which there sprang a demoniacal Counsellor in a black gown, with an obnoxious head of hair, and a red cloth mouth, wide open, who was not to be endured on any terms, but could not be put away either; for he used suddenly, in a highly magnified state, to fly out of Mammoth Snuff-boxes in dreams, when least expected. Nor is the frog with cobbler's wax on his tail, far off; for there was no knowing where he wouldn't jump; and when he flew over the candle, and came upon one's hand with that spotted back—red on a green ground—he was horrible. The cardboard lady in a blue-silk skirt, who was stood up against the candle-stick to dance, and whom I see on the same branch, was milder, and was beautiful; but I can't say as much for the larger cardboard man, who used to be hung against the wall and pulled by a string; there was a sinister expression in that nose of his; and when he got his legs round his neck (which he very often did), he was ghastly, and not a creature to be alone with.

When did that dreadful Mask first look at me? Who put it on, and why was I so frightened that the sight of it is an era in my life. It is not a hideous visage in itself; it is even meant to be droll; why then were its stolid features so intolerable? Surely not because it hid the wearer's face. An apron would have done as much; and though I should have preferred even the apron away, it would not have been absolutely insupportable, like the Mask. Was it the immovability of the Mask? The doll's face was immovable, but I was not afraid of *her*. Perhaps that fixed and set change coming over a real face, infused into my quickened heart some remote suggestion and dread of the universal change that is to come on every face, and make it still? Nothing reconciled me to it. No drummers, from whom proceeded a melancholy chirping on the turning of a handle; no regiment of soldiers, with a mute band, taken out of a box, and fitted, one by one, upon a stiff and lazy little set of lazy-tongs; no old woman, made of wires and a brown-paper composition, cutting up a pie for two small children; could give me a permanent comfort, for a long time. Nor was it any satisfaction to be shown the Mask, and see that it was made of paper, or to have it locked up and be assured that no one wore it. The mere recollection of that fixed face, the mere knowledge of its existence anywhere, was sufficient to wake me in the night all perspiration and horror, with, "O I know it's coming! O the Mask!"

I never wondered what the dear old donkey with the

panniers—there he is! was made of, then! His hide was real to the touch, I recollect. And the great black horse with the round red spots all over him—the horse that I could even get upon—I never wondered what had brought him to that strange condition, or thought that such a horse was not commonly seen at Newmarket. The four horses of no color, next to him, that went into the wagon of cheeses, and could be taken out and stabled under the piano, appear to have bits of fur-tippet for their tails, and other bits for their manes, and to stand on pegs instead of legs, but it was not so when they were brought home for a Christmas present. They were all right, then; neither was their harness unceremoniously nailed into their chests, as appears to be the case now. The tinkling works of the music-cart, I *did* find out, to be made of quill tooth-picks and wire; and I always thought that little tumbler in his shirt sleeves, perpetually swarming up one side of a wooden frame, and coming down, head foremost, on the other, rather a weak-minded person—though good-natured; but the Jacob's Ladder, next him, made of little squares of red wood, that went flapping and clattering over one another, each developing a different picture, and the whole enlivened by small bells, was a mighty marvel and a great delight.

Ah! The Doll's house!—of which I was not proprietor, but where I visited. I don't admire the Houses of Parliament half so much as that stone-fronted mansion with real glass windows, and door-steps, and a real balcony— greener than I ever see now, except at watering places; and even they afford but a poor imitation. And though it *did* open all at once, the entire house-front (which was a blow, I admit, as canceling the fiction of a staircase), it was but to shut it up again, and I could believe. Even open, there were three distinct rooms in it: a sitting-room and bed-room, elegantly furnished, and best of all, a kitchen, with uncommonly soft fire-irons, a plentiful assortment of diminutive utensils—oh, the warming-pan!—and a tin man-cook in profile, who was always going to fry two fish. What Barmecide justice have I done to the noble feasts wherein the set of wooden platters figured, each with its own peculiar delicacy, as a ham or turkey, glued tight on to it, and garnished with something green, which I recollect as moss! Could all the Temperance Societies of these later days, united, give me such a tea-drinking as I have had through the means of yonder little set of blue crockery, which really would hold liquid (it ran out of the small wooden cask, I recollect, and tasted of matches), and which made tea, nectar. And if the two legs of the ineffectual little sugar-tongs did tumble over one another, and want purpose, like Punch's hands, what does it matter? And if I did once shriek out, as a poisoned child, and strike the fashionable company with consternation, by reason of having drunk a little teaspoon, inadvertently dissolved in too hot tea, I was never the worse for it, except by a powder!

Upon the next branches of the tree, lower down, hard by the green roller and miniature gardening-tools, how thick the books begin to hang. Thin books, in themselves, at first, but many of them, and with deliciously smooth covers of bright red or green. What fat black letters to begin with! "A was an archer, and shot at a frog." Of course he was. He was an apple-pie also, and there he is! He was a good many things in his time, was A, and so were most of his friends, except X, who had so little versatility, that I never knew him to get beyond Xerxes or Xantippe—like Y, who was always confined to a Yacht or a Yew Tree; and Z condemned for ever to be a Zebra or a Zany. But, now, the very tree itself changes, and becomes a bean-stalk—the marvelous bean-stalk up which Jack climbed to the Giant's house! And now, those dreadfully interesting, double-headed giants, with their clubs over their shoulders, begin to stride along the boughs in a perfect throng, dragging knights and ladies home for dinner by the hair of their heads. And Jack—how noble, with his sword of sharpness, and his shoes of swiftness! Again those old meditations come upon me as I gaze up at him; and I debate within myself whether there was more than one Jack (which I am loth to believe possible), or only one genuine original admirable Jack, who achieved all the recorded exploits.

Good for Christmas-time is the ruddy color of the cloak, in which—the tree making a forest of itself for her to trip through, with her basket—Little Red Riding-Hood comes to me one Christmas Eve to give me information of the cruelty and treachery of that dissembling Wolf who ate her grandmother, without making any impression on his appetite, and then ate her, after making that ferocious joke about his teeth. She was my first love. I felt that if I could have married Little Red Riding-Hood, I should have known perfect bliss. But, it was not to be; and there was nothing for it but to look out the Wolf in the Noah's Ark there, and put him late in the procession on the table, as a monster who was to be degraded. O the wonderful Noah's Ark! It was not found seaworthy when put in a washing-tub, and the animals were crammed in at the roof, and needed to have their legs well shaken down before they could be got in, even there—and then, ten to one but they began to tumble out at the door, which was but imperfectly fastened with a wire latch—but what was *that* against it! Consider the noble fly, a size or two smaller than the elephant: the lady-bird, the butterfly—all triumphs of art! Consider the goose, whose feet were so small, and whose balance was so indifferent, that he usually tumbled forward, and knocked down all the animal creation. Consider Noah and his family, like idiotic tobacco-stoppers; and how the leopard stuck to warm little fingers; and how the tails of the larger animals used gradually to resolve themselves into frayed bits of string!

Hush! Again a forest, and somebody up in a tree—not Robin Hood, not Valentine, not the Yellow Dwarf (I have passed him and all Mother Bunch's wonders, without mention), but an Eastern King with a glittering scimitar and turban. By Allah! two Eastern Kings, for I see another, looking over his shoulder! Down upon the grass, at the tree's foot, lies the full length of a coal-black Giant, stretched asleep, with his head in a lady's lap; and near them is a glass box, fastened with four locks of shining steel, in which he keeps the lady prisoner when he is awake. I see the four keys at his girdle now. The lady makes signs to the two kings in the trees, who softly descend. It is the setting-in of the bright Arabian Nights.

Oh, now all common things become uncommon and enchanted to me. All lamps are wonderful; all rings are talismans. Common flower-pots are full of treasure, with a little earth scattered on the top; trees are for Ali Baba to hide in; beef-steaks are to throw down into the Valley of Diamonds, that the precious stones may stick to them, and be carried by the eagles to their nests, whence the traders, with loud cries, will scare them. Tarts are made, according to the recipe of the Vizier's son of Bussorah, who turned pastrycook after he was set down in his drawers at the gate of Damascus; cobblers are all Mustaphas, and in the habit of sewing up people cut into four pieces, to whom they are taken blindfold.

Any iron ring let into stone is the entrance to a cave which only waits for the magician, and the little fire, and the necromancy, that will make the earth shake. All the dates imported come from the same tree as that unlucky date, with whose shell the merchant knocked out the eye of the genie's invisible son. All olives are of the stock of that fresh fruit, concerning which the Commander of the Faithful overheard the boy conduct the fictitious trail of the fraudulent olive merchant; all apples are akin to the apple purchased (with two others) from the Sultan's gardener for three sequins, and which the tall black slaves stole from the child. All dogs are associated with the dog, really a transformed man, who jumped upon the baker's counter, and put his paw on the piece of bad money. All rice recalls the rice which the awful lady, who was a ghoule, could only peck by grains, because of her nightly feasts in the burial-place. My very rocking-horse,—there he is, with his nostrils turned completely inside-out, indicative of Blood!—should have a peg in his neck, by virtue thereof to fly away with me, as the wooden horse did with the Prince of Persia, in the sight of all his father's Court.

Yes, on every object that I recognize among those upper branches of my Christmas Tree, I see this fairy light! When I wake in bed, at daybreak, on the cold, dark, winter mornings, the white snow dimly beheld, outside, through the frost on the windowpane, I hear Dinarzade. "Sister, sister, if you are yet awake, I pray you finish the history of the Young King of the Black Islands." Scheherazade replies, "If my lord the Sultan will suffer me to live another day, sister, I will not only finish that, but tell you a more wonderful story yet." Then, the gracious Sultan goes out, giving no orders for the execution, and we all three breathe again.

At this height of my tree I begin to see, cowering among the leaves—it may be born of turkey, or of pudding, or mince pie, or of these many fancies, jumbled with Robinson Crusoe on his desert island, Philip Quarll among the monkeys, Sandford and Merton with Mr. Barlow, Mother Bunch, and the Mask—or it may be the result of indigestion, assisted by imagination and over-doctoring—a prodigious nightmare. It is so exceedingly indistinct, that I don't know why it's frightful—but I know it is. I can only make out that it is an immense array of shapeless things, which appear to be planted on a vast exaggeration of the lazy-tongs that used to bear the toy soldiers, and to be slowly coming close to my eyes, and receding to an immeasurable distance. When it comes closest, it is worse. In connection with it I descry remembrances of winter nights incredibly long; of being sent early to bed, as a punishment for some small offense, and waking in two hours, with a sensation of having been asleep two nights; of the leaden hopelessness of morning ever dawning; and the oppression of a weight of remorse.

And now, I see a wonderful row of little lights rise smoothly out of the ground, before a vast green curtain. Now, a bell rings—a magic bell, which still sounds in my ears unlike all other bells—and music plays, amidst a buzz of voices, and a fragrant smell of orange-peel and oil. Anon, the magic bell commands the music to cease, and the great green curtain rolls itself up majestically, and The Play begins! The devoted dog of Montargis avenges the death of his master, foully murdered in the Forest of Bondy; and a humorous Peasant with a red nose and a very little hat, whom I take from this hour forth to my bosom as a friend (I think he was a Waiter or an Hostler at a village Inn, but many years have passed since he and I have met), remarks that the sassigassity of that dog is indeed surprising; and evermore this jocular conceit will live in my remembrance fresh and unfading, overtopping all possible jokes, unto the end of time. Or now, I learn with bitter tears how poor Jane Shore, dressed all in white, and with her brown hair hanging down, went starving through the streets; or how George Barnwell killed the worthiest uncle that ever man had, and was afterwards so sorry for it that he ought to have been let off. Comes swift to comfort me, the Pantomime—stupendous Phenomenon!—when clowns are shot from loaded mortars into the great chandelier, bright constellation that it is; when Harlequins, covered all over with scales of pure gold, twist and sparkle, like amazing fish; when Pantaloon (whom I deem it no irreverence to compare in my own mind to my grandfather) puts red-hot pokers in his pocket, and cries "Here's somebody coming!" or taxes the Clown with petty larceny, by saying, "Now, I sawed you do it!" when Everything is capable, with the greatest ease, of being changed into Anything; and "Nothing is, but thinking makes it so." Now, too, I perceive my first experience of the dreary sensation—often to return in after-life —of being unable, next day, to get back to the dull, settled world; of wanting to live for ever in the bright atmosphere I have quitted; of doting on the little Fairy, with the wand like a celestial Barber's Pole, and pining for a Fairy immortality along with her. Ah, she comes back, in many shapes, as my eye wanders down the branches of my Christmas Tree, and goes as often, and has never yet stayed by me!

Out of this delight springs the toy-theatre,—there it is, with its familiar proscenium, and ladies in feathers, in the boxes!—and all its attendant occupation with paste and glue, and gum, and water colors, in the getting-up of The Miller and his Men, and Elizabeth, or the Exile of Siberia. In spite of a few besetting accidents and failures (particularly an unreasonable disposition in the respectable Kelmar, and some others, to become faint in the legs, and double up, at exciting points of the drama), a teeming

world of fancies so suggestive and all-embracing, that, far
below it on my Christmas Tree, I see dark, dirty, real
Theaters in the daytime, adorned with these associations
as with the freshest garlands of the rarest flowers, and
charming me yet.

But hark! The Waits are playing, and they break my
childish sleep! What images do I associate with the
Christmas music as I see them set forth on the Christmas
Tree? Known before all the others, keeping far apart from
all the others, they gather round my little bed. An angel,
speaking to a group of shepherds in a field; some travellers, with eyes uplifted, following a star; a baby in a man-
ger; a child in a spacious temple, talking with grave men;
a solemn figure, with a mild and beautiful face, raising a
dead girl by the hand; again, near a city gate, calling back
the son of a widow, on his bier, to life; a crowd of people
looking through the opened roof of a chamber where he
sits, and letting down a sick person on a bed, with ropes;
the same, in a tempest, walking on the water to a ship;
again, on a sea-shore, teaching a great multitude; again,
with a child upon his knee, and other children round;
again, restoring sight to the blind, speech to the dumb,
hearing to the deaf, health to the sick, strength to the
lame, knowledge to the ignorant; again, dying upon a
Cross, watched by armed soldiers, a thick darkness coming on, the earth beginning to shake, and only one voice
heard, "Forgive them, for they know not what they do."

Still, on the lower and maturer branches of the Tree,
Christmas associations cluster thick. School books shut
up; Ovid and Virgil silenced; the Rule of Three, with its

cool impertinent inquiries, long disposed of; Terence and Plautus acted no more, in an arena of huddled desks and forms, all chipped, and notched, and inked; cricket-bats, stumps, and balls, left higher up, with the smell of trodden grass and the softened noise of shouts in the evening air; the tree is still fresh, still gay. If I no more come home at Christmastime, there will be boys and girls (thank Heaven!) while the World lasts; and they do! Yonder they dance and play upon the branches of my Tree, God bless them, merrily, and my heart dances and plays too!

And I *do* come home at Christmas. We all do, or we all should. We all come home, or ought to come home, for a short holiday—the longer, the better—from the great boarding-school, where we are for ever working at our arithmetical slates, to take, and give a rest. As to going a visiting, where can we not go, if we will; where have we not been, when we would; starting our fancy from our Christmas Tree!

Away into the winter prospect. There are many such upon the tree! On, by low-lying, misty grounds, through fens and fogs, up long hills, winding dark as caverns between thick plantations, almost shutting out the sparkling stars; so, out on broad heights, until we stop at last, with sudden silence, at an avenue. The gatebell has a deep, half-awful sound in the frosty air; the gate swings open on its hinges; and, as we drive up to a great house, the glancing lights grow larger in the windows, and the opposing rows of trees seem to fall solemnly back on either side, to give us place. At intervals, all day, a frightened hare has shot across this whitened turf; or the distant clatter of a herd of deer trampling the hard frost, has, for the minute, crushed the silence too. Their watchful eyes beneath the fern may be shining now, if we could see them, like the icy dewdrops on the leaves; but they are still, and all is still. And so, the lights growing larger, and the trees falling back before us, and closing up again behind us, as if to forbid retreat, we come to the house.

There is probably a smell of roasted chestnuts and other good comfortable things all the time, for we are telling Winter Stories—Ghost Stories, or more shame for us— round the Christmas fire; and we have never stirred, except to draw a little nearer to it. But, no matter for that. We come to the house, and it is an old house, full of great chimneys where wood is burnt on ancient dogs upon the hearth, and grim portraits (some of them with grim legends, too) lower distrustfully from the oaken panels of the walls. We are a middle-aged nobleman, and we make a generous supper with our host and hostess and their guests —it being Christmastime, and the old house full of company—and then we go to bed. Our room is a very old room. It is hung with tapestry. We don't like the portrait of a cavalier in green, over the fireplace. There are great black beams in the ceiling, and there is a great black bedstead, supported at the foot by two great black figures, who seem to have come off a couple of tombs in the old baronial church in the park, for our particular accommodation. But, we are not a superstitious nobleman, and we don't mind. Well! we dismiss our servant, lock the door, and sit before the fire in our dressing-gown, musing about a great many things. At length we go to bed. Well! we can't sleep. We toss and tumble, and can't sleep. The embers on the hearth burn fitfully and make the room look ghostly. We can't help peeping out over the counterpane, at the two black figures and the cavalier—that wicked-looking cavalier—in green. In the flickering light they seem to advance and retire: which, though we are not by any means a superstitious nobleman, is not agreeable. Well! we get nervous—more and more nervous. We say "This is very foolish, but we can't stand this; we'll pretend to be ill, and knock up somebody." Well! we are just going to do it, when the locked door opens, and there comes in a young woman, deadly pale, and with long fair hair, who glides to the fire, and sits down in the chair we have left there, wringing her hands. Then, we notice that her clothes are wet. Our tongue cleaves to the roof of our mouth, and we can't speak; but, we observe her accurately. Her clothes are wet; her long hair is dabbled with moist mud; she is dressed in the fashion of two hundred years ago; and she has at her girdle a bunch of rusty keys. Well! there she sits, and we can't even faint, we are in such a state about it. Presently she gets up, and tries all the locks in the room with the rusty keys, which don't fit one of them; then, she fixes her eyes on the portrait of the cavalier in green, and says, in a low, terrible voice, "The stags know it!" After that, she wrings her hands again, passes the bedside, and goes out at the door. We hurry on our dressing-gown, seize our pistols (we always travel with pistols), and are following, when we find the door locked. We turn the key, look out into the dark gallery; no one there. We wander away, and try to find our servant. Can't be done. We pace the gallery till daybreak; then return to our deserted room, fall asleep, and are awakened by our servant (nothing ever haunts *him*) and the shining sun. Well! we make a wretched breakfast, and all the company say we look queer. After breakfast, we go over the house with our host, and then we take him to the portrait of the cavalier in green, and then it all comes out. He was false to a young housekeeper once attached to that family, and famous for her beauty, who drowned herself in a pond, and whose body was discovered, after a long time, because the stags refused to drink of the water. Since which, it has been whispered that she traverses the house at midnight (but goes especially to that room where the cavalier in green was wont to sleep), trying the old locks with the rusty keys. Well! we tell our host of what we have seen, and a shade comes over his features, and he begs it may be hushed up; and so it is. But, it's all true; and we said so, before we died (we are dead now) to many responsible people.

There is no end to the old houses, with resounding galleries, and dismal state-bedchambers, and haunted wings shut up for many years, through which we may ramble, with an agreeable creeping up our back, and encounter any number of ghosts, but (it is worthy of remark perhaps) reducible to a very few general types and classes; for, ghosts have little originality, and "walk" in a beaten track. Thus, it comes to pass, that a certain room in a certain old hall, where a certain bad lord, baronet, knight, or gentleman, shot himself, has certain planks in the floor from which the blood *will not* be taken out. You may scrape and scrape, as the present owner has done, or plane and plane, as his father did, or scrub and scrub, as his grandfather did, or burn and burn with strong acids, as his great-grandfather did, but, there the blood will still be—no redder and no paler—no more and no less—always just the same. Thus, in such another house there is a haunted door, that never will keep open; or another door that never will keep shut; or a haunted sound of a spinning-wheel, or a hammer, or a footstep, or a cry, or a sigh, or a horse's tramp, or the rattling of a chain. Or else, there is a turret-clock, which, at the midnight hour, strikes thirteen when the head of the family is going to die; or a shadowy, immovable black carriage which at such a time is always seen by somebody, waiting near the great gates in the stable-yard. Or thus, it came to pass how Lady Mary went to pay a visit at a large wild house in the Scottish Highlands, and being fatigued with her long journey, retired to bed early, and innocently said, next morning, at the breakfast table, "How odd, to have so late a party last night, in this remote place, and not tell me of it, before I went to bed!" Then, every one asked Lady Mary what she meant? Then, Lady Mary replied, "Why, all night long, the carriages were driving round and round the terrace, underneath my window!" Then, the owner of the house turned pale, and so did his Lady, and Charles Macdoodle of Macdoodle signed to Lady Mary to say no more, and every one was silent. After breakfast, Charles Macdoodle told Lady Mary that it was a tradition in the family that those rumbling carriages on the terrace betokened death. And so it proved, for, two months afterwards, the Lady of the mansion died. And Lady Mary, who was a Maid of Honor at Court, often told this story to the old Queen Charlotte; by this token that the old King always said, "Eh, eh? What, what? Ghosts, ghosts? No such thing, no such thing!" And never left off saying so, until he went to bed.

Or, a friend of somebody's whom most of us know, when he was a young man at college, had a particular friend, with whom he made the compact that, if it were possible for the Spirit to return to this earth after its separation from the body, he of the twain who first died, should reappear to the other. In course of time, this compact was forgotten by our friend; the two young men having progressed in life, and taken diverging paths that were wide asunder. But, one night, many years afterwards, our friend being in the North of England, and staying for the night in an inn, on the Yorkshire Moors, happened to look out of bed; and there, in the moonlight, leaning on a bureau near the window, steadfastly regarding him, saw his old college friend! The appearance being solemnly addressed, replied, in a kind of whisper, but very audibly, "Do not come near me. I am dead. I am here to redeem my promise. I come from another world, but may not disclose its secrets!" Then, the whole form becoming paler, melted, as it were, into the moonlight, and faded away.

Or, there was the daughter of the first occupier of the picturesque Elizabethan house, so famous in our neighborhood. You have heard about her? No! Why *She* went out one summer evening at twilight, when she was a beautiful girl, just seventeen years of age, to gather flowers in the garden; and presently came running, terrified, into the hall to her father, saying, "Oh, dear father, I have met myself!" He took her in his arms, and told her it was fancy, but she said, "Oh, no! I met myself in the broad walk, and I was pale and gathering withered flowers, and I turned my head, and held them up!" And, that night she died; and a picture of her story was begun, though never finished, and they say it is somewhere in the house to this day, with its face to the wall.

Or, the uncle of my brother's wife was riding home on horseback, one mellow evening at sunset, when in a green lane close to his own house, he saw a man standing before him, in the very center of a narrow way. "Why does that man in the cloak stand there!" he thought. "Does he want me to ride over him?" But the figure never moved. He felt a strange sensation at seeing it so still, but slackened his trot and rode forward. When he was so close to it, as almost to touch it with his stirrup, his horse shied, and the figure glided up the bank, in a curious, unearthly manner —backward, and without seeming to use its feet—and was gone. The uncle of my brother's wife, exclaiming, "Good Heaven! It's my cousin Harry, from Bombay!" put spurs to his horse, which was suddenly in a profuse sweat, and, wondering at such strange behavior, dashed round to the front of his house. There, he saw the same figure, just passing in at the long French window of the drawing-room, opening on the ground. He threw his bridle to a servant, and hastened in after it. His sister was sitting there, alone. "Alice, where's my cousin Harry?" "Your cousin Harry, John?" "Yes. From Bombay. I met him in the lane just now, and saw him enter here, this instant." Not a creature had been seen by any one; and in that hour and minute, as it afterwards appeared, this cousin died in India.

Or, it was a certain sensible old maiden lady, who died at ninety-nine, and retained her faculties to the last, who really did see the Orphan Boy; a story which has often been incorrectly told, but, of which the real truth is this—because it is, in fact, a story belonging to our family—and she was a connection of our family. When she was about forty years of age, and still an uncommonly fine woman (her lover died young, which was the reason why she never married, though she had many offers), she went to stay at a place in Kent, which her brother, an Indian-Merchant, had newly bought. There was a story that this place had once been held in trust by the guardian of a young boy; who was himself the next heir, and who killed the young boy by harsh and cruel treatment. She knew nothing of that. It has been said that there was a Cage in her bedroom in which the guardian used to put the boy. There was no such a thing. There was only a closet. She went to bed, made no alarm whatever in the night, and in the morning said composedly to her maid when she came in, "Who is the pretty forlorn-looking child who has been peeping out of that closet all night?" The maid replied by giving a loud scream, and instantly decamping. She was surprised; but she was a woman of remarkable strength of mind, and she dressed herself and went downstairs, and closeted herself with her brother. "Now, Walter," she said, "I have been disturbed all night by a pretty forlorn-looking boy, who has been constantly peeping out of that closet in my room, which I can't open. This is some trick." "I am afraid not, Charlotte," said he, "for it is the legend of the house. It is the Orphan Boy. What did he do?" "He opened the door softly," said she, "and peeped out. Sometimes, he came a step or two into the room. Then, I called to him, to encourage him, and he shrunk, and shuddered, and crept in again, and shut the door." "The closet has no communication, Charlotte," said her brother, "with any other part of the house, and it's nailed up." This was undeniably true, and it took two carpenters a whole forenoon to get it open, for examination. Then, she was satisfied that she had seen the Orphan Boy. But, the wild and terrible part of the story is, that he was also seen by three of her brother's sons, in succession, who all died young. On the occasion of each child being taken ill, he came home in a heat, twelve hours before, and said, "Oh, Mamma, he had been playing under a particular oak tree, in a certain meadow, with a strange boy—a pretty, forlorn-looking boy, who was very timid, and made signs! From fatal experience, the parents came to know that this was the Orphan Boy, and that the course of that child whom he chose for his little playmate was surely run.

Legion is the name of the German castles, where we sit up alone to wait for the Spectre—where we are shown into a room, made comparatively cheerful for our reception—where we glance round at the shadows, thrown on the blank walls by the crackling fire—where we feel very lonely when the village inn-keeper and his pretty daughter have retired, after laying down a fresh store of wood upon

the hearth, and setting forth on the small table such sup-
per-cheer as a cold roast capon, bread, grapes, and a flask
of old Rhine wine—where the reverberating doors close
on their retreat, one after another, like so many peals of
sullen thunder—and where, about the small hours of the
night, we come into the knowledge of divers supernatural
mysteries. Legion is the name of the haunted German stu-
dents, in whose society we draw yet nearer to the fire,
while the schoolboy in the corner opens his eyes wide and
round, and flies off the footstool he has chosen for his seat,
when the door accidentally blows open. Vast is the crop
of such fruit, shining on our Christmas Tree; in blossom,
almost at the very top; ripening all down the boughs!

Among the later toys and fancies hanging there—as idle
often and less pure—be the images once associated with
the sweet old Waits, the softened music in the night, ever
unalterable! Encircled by the social thoughts of Christmastime, still let the benignant figure of my childhood
stand unchanged! In every cheerful image and suggestion
that the season brings, may the bright star that rested
above the poor roof, be the star of all the Christian
World! A moment's pause, O vanishing tree, of which the
lower boughs are dark to me as yet, and let me look once
more! I know there are blank spaces on thy branches,
where eyes that I have loved have shone and smiled; from
which they are departed. But, far above, I see the raiser of
the dead girl, and the Widow's Son; and God is good! If
Age be hiding for me in the unseen portion of thy downward growth, O may I, with a grey head, turn a child's

heart to that figure yet, and a child's trustfulness and confidence!

Now, the tree is decorated with bright merriment, and song, and dance, and cheerfulness. And they are welcome. Innocent and welcome be they ever held, beneath the branches of the Christmas Tree, which cast no gloomy shadow! But, as it sinks into the ground, I hear a whisper going through the leaves. "This, in commemoration of the law of love and kindness, mercy and compassion. This, in remembrance of Me!"

WHAT CHRISTMAS IS AS WE GROW OLDER

ime was, with most of us, when Christmas Day encircling all our limited world like a magic ring, left nothing out for us to miss or seek; bound together all our home enjoyments, affections, and hopes; grouped everything and every one around the Christmas fire; and made the little picture shining in our bright young eyes, complete.

Time came, perhaps, all so soon, when our thoughts overleaped that narrow boundary; when there was some one (very dear, we thought then, very beautiful, and absolutely perfect) wanting to the fulness of our happiness; when we were wanting too (or we thought so, which did just as well) at the Christmas hearth by which that some one sat; and when we intertwined with every wreath and garland of our life that some one's name.

That was the time for the bright visionary Christmases which have long arisen from us to show faintly, after summer rain, in the palest edges of the rainbow! That was the time for the beatified enjoyment of the things that were to be, and never were, and yet the things that were so real in our resolute hope that it would be hard to say, now, what realities achieved since, have been stronger!

What! Did that Christmas never really come when we and the priceless pearl who was our young choice were received, after the happiest of totally impossible marriages, by the two united families previously at daggers-drawn on our account? When brothers and sisters-in-law who had always been rather cool to us before our relationship was effected, perfectly doted on us, and when fathers and mothers overwhelmed us with unlimited incomes? Was that Christmas dinner never really eaten, after which we arose, and generously and eloquently rendered honor to our late rival, present in the company, then and there exchanging friendship and forgiveness, and founding an attachment, not to be surpassed in Greek or Roman story, which subsisted until death? Has that same rival long ceased to care for that same priceless pearl, and married for money, and become usurious? Above all, do we really know, now, that we should probably have been miserable if we had won and worn the pearl, and that we are better without her?

That Christmas when we had recently achieved so much fame; when we had been carried in triumph somewhere, for doing something great and good; when we had won an honored and ennobled name, and arrived and were received at home in a shower of tears of joy; is it possible that *that* Christmas has not come yet?

And is our life here, at the best, so constituted that,

pausing as we advance at such a noticeable mile-stone in the track as this great birthday, we look back on the things that never were, as naturally and full as gravely as on the things that have been and are gone, or have been and still are? If it be so, and so it seems to be, must we come to the conclusion that life is little better than a dream, and little worth the loves and strivings that we crowd into it?

No! Far be such miscalled philosophy from us, dear Reader, on Christmas Day! Nearer and closer to our hearts be the Christmas spirit, which is the spirit of active usefulness, perseverance, cheerful discharge of duty, kindness and forbearance! It is in the last virtues especially, that we are, or should be, strengthened by the unaccomplished visions of our youth; for, who shall say that they are not our teachers to deal gently even with the impalpable nothings of the earth!

Therefore, as we grow older, let us be more thankful that the circle of our Christmas associations and of the lessons that they bring, expands! Let us welcome every one of them, and summon them to take their places by the Christmas hearth.

Welcome, old aspirations, glittering creatures of an ardent fancy, to your shelter underneath the holly! We know you, and have not outlived you yet. Welcome, old projects and old loves, however fleeting, to your nooks among the steadier lights that burn around us. Welcome, all that was ever real to our hearts; and for the earnestness that made you real, thanks to Heaven! Do we build no Christmas castles in the clouds now? Let our thoughts, fluttering like butterflies among these flowers of children, bear witness! Before this boy, there stretches out a Future, brighter than we ever looked on in our old romantic time, but bright with honor and with truth. Around this little head on which the sunny curls lie heaped, the graces sport, as prettily, as airily, as when there was no scythe within the reach of Time to shear away the curls of our first-love. Upon another girl's face near it—placider but smiling bright—a quiet and contented little face, we see Home fairly written. Shining from the word, as rays shine from a star, we see how, when our graves are old, other hopes than ours are young, other hearts than ours are moved; how other ways are smoothed; how other happiness blooms, ripens, and decays—no, not decays, for other homes and other bands of children, not yet in being nor for ages yet to be, arise, and bloom and ripen to the end of all!

Welcome, everything! Welcome, alike what has been, and what never was, and what we hope may be, to your shelter underneath the holly, to your places round the Christmas fire, where what is sits open-hearted! In yonder shadow, do we see obtruding furtively upon the blaze, an enemy's face? By Christmas Day we do forgive him! If the injury he has done us may admit of such companionship, let him come here and take his place. If otherwise, unhappily, let him go hence, assured that we will never injure nor accuse him.

On this day we shut out Nothing!

"Pause," says a low voice. "Nothing? Think!"

"On Christmas Day, we will shut out from our fireside, Nothing."

"Not the shadow of a vast City where the withered leaves are lying deep?" the voice replies. "Not the shadow that darkens the whole globe? Not the shadow of the City of the Dead?"

Not even that. Of all days in the year, we will turn our faces towards that City upon Christmas Day, and from its silent hosts bring those we loved, among us. City of the Dead, in the blessed name wherein we are gathered together at this time, and in the Presence that is here among us according to the promise, we will receive, and not dismiss, thy people who are dear to us!

Yes. We can look upon these children angels that alight, so solemnly, so beautifully among the living children by the fire, and can bear to think how they departed from us. Entertaining angels unawares, as the Patriarchs did, the playful children are unconscious of their guests; but we can see them—can see a radiant arm around one favorite neck, as if there were a tempting of that child away. Among the celestial figures there is one, a poor misshapen boy on earth, of a glorious beauty now, of whom his dying mother said it grieved her much to leave him here, alone, for so many years as it was likely would elapse before he came to her—being such a little child. But he went quickly, and was laid upon her breast, and in her hand she leads him.

There was a gallant boy, who fell, far away, upon a burning sand 'beneath a burning sun, and said, "Tell them at home, with my last love, how much I could have wished to kiss them once, but that I died contented and had done my duty!" Or there was another, over whom they read the words, "Therefore we commit his body to the deep," and so consigned him to the lonely ocean and sailed on. Or there was another, who lay down to his rest in the dark shadow of great forests, and, on earth, awoke no more. O shall they not, from sand and sea and forest, be brought home at such a time!

There was a dear girl—almost a woman—never to be one—who made a mourning Christmas in a house of joy, and went her trackless way to the silent City. Do we recollect her, worn out, faintly whispering what could not be heard, and falling into that last sleep for weariness? O look upon her now! O look upon her beauty, her serenity, her changeless youth, her happiness! The daughter of Jairus was recalled to life, to die; but she, more blest, has heard the same voice, saying unto her, "Arise for ever!"

We had a friend who was our friend from early days, with whom we often pictured the changes that were to come upon our lives, and merrily imagined how we would speak, and walk, and think, and talk, when we came to be old. His destined habitation in the City of the Dead received him in his prime. Shall he be shut out from our Christmas remembrance? Would his love have so excluded us? Lost friend, lost child, lost parent, sister, brother, husband, wife, we will not so discard you! You shall hold your cherished places in our Christmas hearts, and by our Christmas fires; and in the season of immortal hope, and on the birthday of immortal mercy, we will shut out Nothing!

The winter sun goes down over town and village; on the sea it makes a rosy path, as if the Sacred tread were fresh upon the water. A few more moments, and it sinks, and night comes on, and lights begin to sparkle in the prospect. On the hillside beyond the shapelessly-diffused town, and in the quiet keeping of the trees that gird the village steeple, remembrances are cut in stone, planted in common flowers, growing in grass, entwined with lowly brambles around many a mound of earth. In town and village, there are doors and windows closed against the weather, there are flaming logs heaped high, there are joyful faces, there is healthy music of voices. Be all ungentleness and harm excluded from the temples of the Household Gods, but be those remembrances admitted with tender encouragement! They are of the time and all its comforting and peaceful reassurances; and of the history that reunited even upon earth the living and the dead; and of the broad beneficence and goodness that too many men have tried to tear to narrow shreds.

THE POOR
RELATION'S STORY

H e was very reluctant to take precedence of so many respected members of the family, by beginning the round of stories they were to relate as they sat in a goodly circle by the Christmas fire; and he modestly suggested that it would be more correct if "John our esteemed host" (whose health he begged to drink) would have the kindness to begin. For as to himself, he said, he was so little used to lead the way that really— But as they all cried out here, that he must begin, and agreed with one voice that he might, could, would, and should begin, he left off rubbing his hands, and took his legs out from under his armchair, and did begin.

I have no doubt (said the poor relation) that I shall surprise the assembled members of our family, and particularly John our esteemed host to whom we are so much indebted for the great hospitality with which he has this day entertained us, by the confession I am going to make.

But, if you do me the honor to be surprised at anything that falls from a person so unimportant in the family as I am, I can only say that I shall be scrupulously accurate in all I relate.

I am not what I am supposed to be. I am quite another thing. Perhaps before I go further, I had better glance at what I *am* supposed to be.

It is supposed, unless I mistake—the assembled members of our family will correct me if I do, which is very likely (here the poor relation looked mildly about him for contradiction); that I am nobody's enemy but my own. That I never met with any particular success in anything. That I failed in business because I was unbusinesslike and credulous—in not being prepared for the interested designs of my partner. That I failed in love, because I was ridiculously trustful—in thinking it impossible that Christiana could deceive me. That I failed in my expectations from my uncle Chill, on account of not being as sharp as he could have wished in worldly matters. That, through life, I have been rather put upon and disappointed in a general way. That I am at present a bachelor of between fifty-nine and sixty years of age, living on a limited income in the form of a quarterly allowance, to which I see that John our esteemed host wishes me to make no further allusion.

The supposition as to my present pursuits and habits is to the following effect.

I live in a lodging in the Clapham Road—a very clean back room, in a very respectable house—where I am expected not to be at home in the daytime, unless poorly;

and which I usually leave in the morning at nine o'clock, on pretense of going to business. I take my breakfast—my roll and butter, and my half-pint of coffee—at the old-established coffee-shop near Westminster Bridge; and then I go into the City—I don't know why—and sit in Garraway's Coffee House, and on 'Change, and walk about, and look into a few offices and counting-houses where some of my relations or acquaintance are so good as to tolerate me, and where I stand by the fire if the weather happens to be cold. I get through the day in this way until five o'clock, and then I dine: at a cost, on the average, of one and threepence. Having still a little money to spend on my evening's entertainment, I look into the old-established coffee-shop as I go home, and take my cup of tea, and perhaps my bit of toast. So, as the large hand of the clock makes its way round to the morning hour again, I make my way round to the Clapham Road again, and go to bed when I get to my lodging—fire being expensive, and being objected to by the family on account of its giving trouble and making a dirt.

Sometimes, one of my relations or acquaintances is so obliging as to ask me to dinner. Those are holiday occasions, and then I generally walk in the Park. I am a solitary man, and seldom walk with anybody. Not that I am avoided because I am shabby; for I am not at all shabby, having always a very good suit of black on (or rather Oxford mixture, which has the appearance of black and wears much better); but I have got into a habit of speaking low, and being rather silent, and my spirits are not high, and I am sensible that I am not an attractive companion.

The only exception to this general rule is the child of my first cousin, Little Frank. I have a particular affection for that child, and he takes very kindly to me. He is a diffident boy by nature; and in a crowd he is soon run over, as I may say, and forgotten. He and I, however, get on exceedingly well. I have a fancy that the poor child will in time succeed to my peculiar position in the family. We talk but little; still, we understand each other. We walk about, hand in hand; and without much speaking he knows what I mean, and I know what he means. When he was very little indeed, I used to take him to the windows of the toy-shops, and show him the toys inside. It is surprising how soon he found out that I would have made him a great many presents if I had been in circumstances to do it.

Little Frank and I go and look at the outside of the Monument—he is very fond of the Monument—and at the Bridges, and at all the sights that are free. On two of my birthdays, we have dined on à-la-mode beef, and gone at half-price to the play, and been deeply interested. I was once walking with him in Lombard Street, which we often visit on account of my having mentioned to him that there are great riches there—he is very fond of Lombard Street—when a gentleman said to me as he passed by, "Sir, your little son has dropped his glove." I assure you, if you will excuse my remarking on so trivial a circumstance, this accidental mention of the child as mine, quite

touched my heart and brought the foolish tears into my
eyes.

When Little Frank is sent to school in the country, I
shall be very much at a loss what to do with myself, but I
have the intention of walking down there once a month
and seeing him on a half holiday. I am told he will then be
at play upon the Heath; and if my visits should be objected to, as unsettling the child, I can see him from a
distance without his seeing me, and walk back again. His
mother comes of a highly genteel family, and rather disap-
proves, I am aware, of our being too much together. I
know that I am not calculated to improve his retiring
disposition; but I think he would miss me beyond the feeling of the moment if we were wholly separated.

When I die in the Clapham Road, I shall not leave
much more in this world than I shall take out of it; but, I
happen to have a miniature of a bright-faced boy, with a
curling head, and an open shirt-frill waving down his bosom (my mother had it taken for me, but I can't believe
that it was ever like), which will be worth nothing to sell,
and which I shall beg may be given to Frank. I have
written my dear boy a little letter with it, in which I have
told him that I felt very sorry to part from him, though
bound to confess that I knew no reason why I should
remain here. I have given him some short advice, the best
in my power, to take warning of the consequences of being
nobody's enemy but his own; and I have endeavored to
comfort him for what I fear he will consider a bereavement, by pointing out to him, that I was only a superflu-
ous something to every one but him; and that having by

some means failed to find a place in this great assembly, I am better out of it.

Such (said the poor relation, clearing his throat and beginning to speak a little louder) is the general impression about me. Now, it is a remarkable circumstance which forms the aim and purpose of my story, that this is all wrong. This is not my life, and these are not my habits. I do not even live in the Clapham Road. Comparatively speaking, I am very seldom there. I reside, mostly, in a—I am almost ashamed to say the word, it sounds so full of pretension—in a Castle. I do not mean that it is an old baronial habitation, but still it is a building always known to every one by the name of a Castle. In it, I preserve the particulars of my history; they run thus:

It was when I first took John Spatter (who had been my clerk) into partnership, and when I was still a young man of not more than five-and-twenty, residing in the house of my uncle Chill, from whom I had considerable expectations, that I ventured to propose to Christiana. I had loved Christiana a long time. She was very beautiful, and very winning in all respects. I rather mistrusted her widowed mother, who I feared was of a plotting and mercenary turn of mind; but, I thought as well of her as I could, for Christiana's sake. I never had loved any one but Christiana, and she had been all the world, and O far more than all the world, to me, from our childhood!

Christiana accepted me with her mother's consent, and I was rendered very happy indeed. My life at my uncle Chill's was of a spare dull kind, and my garret chamber was as dull, and bare, and cold, as an upper prison room in some stern northern fortress. But, having Christiana's love, I wanted nothing upon earth. I would not have changed my lot with any human being.

Avarice was, unhappily, my uncle Chill's master-vice. Though he was rich, he pinched, and scraped, and clutched, and lived miserably. As Christiana had no fortune, I was for some time a little fearful of confessing our engagement to him; but, at length I wrote him a letter, saying how it all truly was. I put it into his hand one night, on going to bed.

As I came downstairs next morning, shivering in the cold December air; colder in my uncle's unwarmed house than in the street, where the winter sun did sometimes shine, and which was at all events enlivened by cheerful faces and voices passing along; I carried a heavy heart towards the long low breakfast-room in which my uncle sat. It was a large room with a small fire, and there was a great bay window in it which the rain had marked in the night as if with the tears of houseless people. It stared upon a raw yard, with a cracked stone pavement, and some rusted iron railings half uprooted, whence an ugly out-building that had once been a dissecting-room (in the time of the great surgeon who had mortgaged the house to my uncle), stared at it.

We rose so early always, that at that time of the year we breakfasted by candle-light. When I went into the room, my uncle was so contracted by the cold, and so huddled together in his chair behind the one dim candle, that I did not see him until I was close to the table.

As I held out my hand to him, he caught up his stick

(being infirm, he always walked about the house with a stick), and made a blow at me, and said, "You fool!"

"Uncle," I returned, "I didn't expect you to be so angry as this." Nor had I expected it, though he was a hard and angry old man.

"You didn't expect!" said he; "when did you ever expect? When did you ever calculate, or look forward, you contemptible dog?"

"These are hard words, uncle!"

"Hard words? Feathers, to pelt such an idiot as you with," said he. "Here! Betsy Snap! Look at him!"

Betsy Snap was a withered, hard-favored, yellow old woman—our only domestic—always employed, at this time of the morning, in rubbing my uncle's legs. As my uncle adjured her to look at me, he put his lean grip on the crown of her head, she kneeling beside him, and turned her face towards me. An involuntary thought connecting them both with the Dissecting Room, as it must often have been in the surgeon's time, passed across my mind in the midst of my anxiety.

"Look at the snivelling milksop!" said my uncle. "Look at the baby! This is the gentleman who, people say, is nobody's enemy but his own. This is the gentleman who can't say no. This is the gentleman who was making such large profits in his business that he must needs take a partner, t' other day. This is the gentleman who is going to marry a wife without a penny, and who falls into the hands of Jezabels who are speculating on my death!"

I knew, now, how great my uncle's rage was; for nothing short of his being almost beside himself would have

induced him to utter that concluding word, which he held
in such repugnance that it was never spoken or hinted at
before him on any account.

"On my death," he repeated, as if he were defying me
by defying his own abhorrence of the word. "On my death
—death—Death! But I'll spoil the speculation. Eat your
last under this roof, you feeble wretch, and may it choke
you!"

You may suppose that I had not much appetite for the
breakfast to which I was bidden in these terms; but, I
took my accustomed seat. I saw that I was repudiated
henceforth by my uncle; still I could bear that very well,
possessing Christiana's heart.

He emptied his basin of bread and milk as usual, only
that he took it on his knees with his chair turned away
from the table where I sat. When he had done, he care-
fully snuffed out the candle; and the cold, slate-colored,
miserable day looked in upon us.

"Now, Mr. Michael," said he, "before we part, I
should like to have a word with these ladies in your presence."

"As you will, sir," I returned; "but you deceive yourself, and wrong us, cruelly, if you suppose that there is any
feeling at stake in this contract but pure, disinterested,
faithful love."

To this, he only replied, "You lie!" and not one other
word.

We went, through half-thawed snow and half-frozen
rain, to the house where Christiana and her mother lived.

My uncle knew them very well. They were sitting at their breakfast, and were surprised to see us at that hour.

"Your servant, ma'am," said my uncle to the mother. "You divine the purpose of my visit, I dare say, ma'am. I understand there is a world of pure, disinterested, faithful love cooped up here. I am happy to bring it all it wants, to make it complete. I bring you your son-in-law, ma'am— and you, your husband, miss. The gentleman is a perfect stranger to me, but I wish him joy of his wise bargain."

He snarled at me as he went out, and I never saw him again.

It is altogether a mistake (continued the poor relation) to suppose that my dear Christiana, over-persuaded and in- fluenced by her mother, married a rich man, the dirt from whose carriage wheels is often, in these changed times, thrown upon me as she rides by. No, no. She married me.

The way we came to be married rather sooner than we intended, was this. I took a frugal lodging and was saving and planning for her sake, when, one day, she spoke to me with great earnestness, and said:

"My dear Michael, I have given you my heart. I have said that I loved you, and I have pledged myself to be your wife. I am as much yours through all changes of good and evil as if we had been married on the day when such words passed between us. I know you well, and know that if we should be separated and our union broken off, your whole life would be shadowed, and all that might, even now, be stronger in your character for the conflict with the world would then be weakened to the shadow of what it is!"

"God help me, Christiana!" said I. "You speak the truth."

"Michael!" said she, putting her hand in mine, in all maidenly devotion, "let us keep apart no longer. It is but for me to say that I can live contented upon such means as you have, and I well know you are happy. I say so from my heart. Strive no more alone; let us strive together. My dear Michael, it is not right that I should keep secret from you what you do not suspect, but what distresses my whole life. My mother: without considering that what you have lost, you have lost for me, and on the assurance of my faith: sets her heart on riches, and urges another suit upon me, to my misery. I cannot bear this, for to bear it is to be untrue to you. I would rather share your struggles than look on. I want no better home than you can give me. I know that you will aspire and labor with a higher courage if I am wholly yours, and let it be so when you will!"

I was blest indeed, that day, and a new world opened to me. We were married in a very little while, and I took my wife to our happy home. That was the beginning of the residence I have spoken of; the Castle we have ever since inhabited together, dates from that time. All our children have been born in it. Our first child—now married—was a little girl, whom we called Christiana. Her son is so like Little Frank, that I hardly know which is which.

* * *

The current impression as to my partner's dealings with me is also quite erroneous. He did not begin to treat me coldly, as a poor simpleton, when my uncle and I so fatally quarreled; nor did he afterwards gradually possess himself of our business and edge me out. On the contrary, he behaved to me with the utmost good faith and honor.

Matters between us took this turn:—On the day of my separation from my uncle, and even before the arrival at our countinghouse of my trunks (which he sent after me, *not* carriage paid), I went down to our room of business, on our little wharf, overlooking the river; and there I told John Spatter what had happened. John did not say, in reply, that rich old relatives were palpable facts, and that love and sentiment were moonshine and fiction. He addressed me thus:

"Michael," said John, "we were at school together, and I generally had the knack of getting on better than you, and making a higher reputation."

"You had, John," I returned.

"Although," said John, "I borrowed your books and lost them; borrowed your pocket-money, and never repaid it; got you to buy my damaged knives at a higher price than I had given for them new; and to own to the windows that I had broken."

"All not worth mentioning, John Spatter," said I, "but certainly true."

"When you were first established in this infant business, which promises to thrive so well," pursued John, "I came to you, in my search for almost any employment, and you made me your clerk."

"Still not worth mentioning, my dear John Spatter," said I; "still, equally true."

"And finding that I had a good head for business, and that I was really useful *to* the business, you did not like to retain me in that capacity, and thought it an act of justice soon to make me your partner."

"Still less worth mentioning than any of those other little circumstances you have recalled, John Spatter," said I; "for I was, and am, sensible of your merits and my deficiencies."

"Now, my good friend," said John, drawing my arm through his, as he had had a habit of doing at school; while two vessels outside the windows of our counting-house—which were shaped like the stern windows of a ship—went lightly down the river with the tide, as John and I might then be sailing away in company, and in trust and confidence, on our voyage of life; "let there, under these friendly circumstances, be a right understanding between us. You are too easy, Michael. You are nobody's enemy but your own. If I were to give you that damaging character among our connexion, with a shrug, and a shake of the head, and a sigh; and if I were further to abuse the trust you place in me—"

"But you never will abuse it at all, John," I observed.

"Never!" said he; "but I am putting a case—I say, and if I were further to abuse that trust by keeping this piece of our common affairs in the dark, and this other piece in the light, and again this other piece in the twilight, and so on, I should strengthen my strength, and weaken your weakness, day by day, until at last I found myself on the high road to fortune, and you left behind on some bare common, a hopeless number of miles out of the way."

"Exactly so," said I.

"To prevent this, Michael," said John Spatter, "or the remotest chance of this, there must be perfect openness between us. Nothing must be concealed, and we must have but one interest."

"My dear John Spatter," I assured him, "that is precisely what I mean."

"And when you are too easy," pursued John, his face glowing with friendship, "you must allow me to prevent that imperfection in your nature from being taken advantage of, by any one; you must not expect me to humor it—"

"My dear John Spatter," I interrupted, "I *don't* expect you to humor it. I want to correct it."

"And I, too," said John.

"Exactly so!" cried I. "We both have the same end in view; and, honorably seeking it, and fully trusting one another, and having but one interest, ours will be a prosperous and happy partnership."

"I am sure of it!" returned John Spatter. And we shook hands most affectionately.

I took John home to my Castle, and we had a very happy day. Our partnership throve well. My friend and partner supplied what I wanted, as I had foreseen that he would; and by improving both the business and myself, amply acknowledged any little rise in life to which I had helped him.

* * *

I am not (said the poor relation, looking at the fire as he slowly rubbed his hands) very rich, for I never cared to be that; but I have enough, and am above all moderate wants and anxieties. My Castle is not a splendid place, but it is very comfortable, and it has a warm and cheerful air, and is quite a picture of Home.

Our eldest girl, who is very like her mother, married John Spatter's eldest son. Our two families are closely united in other ties of attachment. It is very pleasant of an evening, when we are all assembled together—which frequently happens—and when John and I talk over old times, and the one interest there has always been between us.

I really do not know, in my Castle, what loneliness is. Some of our children or grandchildren are always about it, and the young voices of my descendants are delightful— O, how delightful!—to me to hear. My dearest and most devoted wife, ever faithful, ever loving, ever helpful and sustaining and consoling, is the priceless blessing of my house; from whom all its other blessings spring. We are rather a musical family, and when Christiana sees me, at any time, a little weary or depressed, she steals to the piano and sings a gentle air she used to sing when we were first betrothed. So weak a man am I, that I cannot bear to hear it from any other source. They played it once, at the Theatre, when I was there with Little Frank; and the child said wondering, "Cousin Michael, whose hot tears are these that have fallen on my hand!"

Such is my Castle, and such are the real particulars of my life therein preserved. I often take Little Frank home there. He is very welcome to my grandchildren, and they play together. At this time of the year—the Christmas and New Year time—I am seldom out of my Castle. For, the associations of the season seem to hold me there, and the precepts of the season seem to teach me that it is well to be there.

"And the Castle is—" observed a grave, kind voice among the company.

"Yes. My Castle," said the poor relation, shaking his head as he still looked at the fire, "is in the Air. John our esteemed host suggests its situation accurately. My Castle is in the Air! I have done. Will you be so good as to pass the story?"

THE CHILD'S STORY

nce upon a time, a good many years ago, there was a traveller, and he set out upon a journey. It was a magic journey, and was to seem very long when he began it, and very short when he got half way through.

He travelled along a rather dark path for some little time, without meeting anything, until at last he came to a beautiful child. So he said to the child, "What do you do here?" And the child said, "I am always at play. Come and play with me!"

So, he played with that child, the whole day long, and they were very merry. The sky was so blue, the sun was so bright, the water was so sparkling, the leaves were so green, the flowers were so lovely, and they heard such singing-birds and saw so many butterflies, that everything was beautiful. This was in fine weather. When it rained, they loved to watch the falling drops, and to smell the fresh scents. When it blew, it was delightful to listen to the wind, and fancy what it said, as it came rushing from its home—where was that, they wondered! —whistling and howling, driving the clouds before it, bending the trees, rumbling in the chimneys, shaking the house, and making the sea roar in fury. But, when it snowed, that was the best of all; for, they liked nothing so well as to look up at the white flakes, falling fast and thick, like down from the breasts of millions of white birds; and to see how smooth and deep the drift was and listen to the hush upon the paths and roads.

They had plenty of the finest toys in the world, and the most astonishing picture-books: all about scimitars and slippers and turbans, and dwarfs and giants and genii and fairies, and blue-beards and bean-stalks and riches and caverns and forests and Valentines and Orsons: and all new and all true.

But, one day, of a sudden, the traveller lost the child. He called to him over and over again, but got no answer. So, he went upon his road, and went on for a little while without meeting anything, until at last he came to a hand-some boy. So, he said to the boy, "What do you do here?" And the boy said, "I am always learning. Come and learn with me."

So he learned with that boy about Jupiter and Juno, and the Greeks and the Romans, and I don't know what, and learned more than I could tell—or he either, for he soon forgot a great deal of it. But, they were not always learn-ing; they had the merriest games that ever were played. They rowed upon the river in summer, and skated on the ice in winter; they were active afoot, and active on horseback, at cricket, and all games at ball; at prisoners' base, hare and hounds, follow my leader, and more sports than I can think of; nobody could beat them. They had holidays too, and Twelfth cakes, and parties where they danced till midnight, and real Theatres where they saw palaces of real gold and silver rise out of the real earth, and saw all the wonders of the world at once. As to friends, they had such dear friends and so many of them, that I want the time to reckon them up. They were all young, like the handsome boy, and were never to be strange to one another again.

Still, one day, in the midst of all these pleasures, the traveller lost the boy as he had lost the child, and, after calling to him in vain, went on upon his journey. So he went on for a little while without seeing anything, until at last he came to a young man. So, he said to the young man, "What do you do here?" And the young man said, "I am always in love. Come and love with me."

So, he went away with that young man, and presently they came to one of the prettiest girls that ever was seen— just like Fanny in the corner there—and she had eyes like Fanny, and hair like Fanny, and dimples like Fanny's, and she laughed and colored just as Fanny does while I am talking about her. So, the young man fell in love directly —just as Somebody I won't mention, the first time he came here, did with Fanny. Well! he was teased some- times—just as Somebody used to be by Fanny; and they quarreled sometimes—just as Somebody and Fanny used to quarrel; and they made it up, and sat in the dark, and wrote letters every day, and never were happy asunder, and were always looking out for one another and pretending not to, and were engaged at Christmastime, and sat close to one another by the fire, and were going to be married very soon—all exactly like Somebody I won't mention, and Fanny!

But, the traveller lost them one day, as he had lost the rest of his friends, and, after calling to them to come back, which they never did, went on upon his journey. So, he went on for a little while without seeing anything, until at last he came to a middleaged gentleman. So, he said to the gentleman, "What are you doing here?" And his answer was, "I am always busy. Come and be busy with me!"

So, he began to be very busy with that gentleman, and they went on through the wood together. The whole journey was through a wood, only it had been open and green at first, like a wood in spring; and now began to be thick and dark, like a wood in summer; some of the little trees that had come out earliest, were even turning brown. The gentleman was not alone, but had a lady of about the same age with him, who was his Wife; and they had children, who were with them too. So, they all went on together through the wood, cutting down the trees, and making a path through the branches and the fallen leaves, and carrying burdens, and working hard.

Sometimes, they came to a long green avenue that opened into deeper woods. Then they would hear a very little, distant voice crying, "Father, father, I am another child! Stop for me!" And presently they would see a very little figure, growing larger as it came along, running to join them. When it came up, they all crowded round it, and kissed and welcomed it; and then they all went on together.

Sometimes, they came to several avenues at once, and then they all stood still, and one of the children said, "Father, I am going to sea," and another said, "Father, I am going to India," and another, "Father, I am going to seek my fortune where I can," and another, "Father, I am going to Heaven!" So, with many tears at parting, they went, solitary, down those avenues, each child upon its way; and the child who went to Heaven, rose into the golden air and vanished.

Whenever these partings happened, the traveller looked at the gentleman, and saw him glance up at the sky above the trees, where the day was beginning to decline, and the sunset to come on. He saw, too, that his hair was turning grey. But, they never could rest long, for they had their journey to perform, and it was necessary for them to be always busy.

At last, there had been so many partings that there were no children left, and only the traveller, the gentleman, and the lady, went upon their way in company. And now the wood was yellow; and now brown; and the leaves, even of the forest trees, began to fall.

So, they came to an avenue that was darker than the rest, and were pressing forward on their journey without looking down it when the lady stopped.

"My husband," said the lady. "I am called."

They listened, and they heard a voice a long way down the avenue, say, "Mother, mother!"

It was the voice of the first child who had said, "I am going to Heaven!" and the father said, "I pray not yet. The sunset is very near. I pray not yet!"

But, the voice cried, "Mother, mother!" without minding him, though his hair was now quite white, and tears were on his face.

Then, the mother, who was already drawn into the shade of the dark avenue and moving away with her arms still round his neck, kissed him, and said, "My dearest, I am summoned, and I go!" And she was gone. And the traveller and he were left alone together.

And they went on and on together, until they came to very near the end of the wood: so near, that they could see the sunset shining red before them through the trees.

Yet, once more, while he broke his way among the branches, the traveller lost his friend. He called and called, but there was no reply, and when he passed out of the wood, and saw the peaceful sun going down upon a wide purple prospect, he came to an old man sitting on a fallen tree. So, he said to the old man, "What do you do here?" And the old man said with a calm smile, "I am always remembering. Come and remember with me!"

So the traveller sat down by the side of that old man, face to face with the serene sunset; and all his friends came softly back and stood around him. The beautiful child, the handsome boy, the young man in love, the father, mother, and children: every one of them was there, and he had lost nothing. So, he loved them all, and was kind and forbearing with them all, and was always pleased to watch them all, and they all honored and loved him. And I think the traveller must be yourself, dear Grandfather, because this is what you do to us, and what we do to you.

THE SCHOOLBOY'S STORY

eing rather young at present—I am getting on in years, but still I am rather young—I have no particular adventures of my own to fall back upon. It wouldn't much interest anybody here, I suppose, to know what a screw the Reverend is, or what a griffin *she* is, or how they do stick it into parents—particularly hair-cutting, and medical attendance. One of our fellows was charged in his half's account twelve and sixpence for two pills—tolerably profitable at six and threepence a-piece, I should think —and he never took them either, but put them up the sleeve of his jacket.

As to the beef, it's shameful. It's *not* beef. Regular beef isn't veins. You can chew regular beef. Besides which, there's gravy to regular beef, and you never see a drop to ours. Another of our fellows went home ill, and heard the family doctor tell his father that he couldn't account for his complaint unless it was the beer. Of course it was the beer, and well it might be!

However, beef and Old Cheeseman are two different things. So is beer. It was Old Cheeseman I meant to tell about; not the manner in which our fellows get their constitutions destroyed for the sake of profit.

Why, look at the pie-crust alone. There's no flakiness in it. It's solid—like damp lead. Then our fellows get nightmares, and are bolstered for calling out and waking other fellows. Who can wonder!

Old Cheeseman one night walked in his sleep, put his hat on over his night-cap, got hold of a fishing-rod and a cricket-bat, and went down into the parlour, where they naturally thought from his appearance he was a Ghost. Why, he never would have done that if his meals had been wholesome. When we all begin to walk in our sleeps, I suppose they'll be sorry for it.

Old Cheeseman wasn't second Latin Master then; he was a fellow himself. He was first brought here, very small, in a post-chaise, by a woman who was always taking snuff and shaking him—and that was the most he remembered about it. He never went home for the holidays. His accounts (he never learnt any extras) were sent to a Bank, and the Bank paid them; and he had a brown suit twice a-year, and went into boots at twelve. They were always too big for him, too.

In the Midsummer holidays, some of our fellows who lived within walking distance, used to come back and climb the trees outside the playground wall, on purpose to look at Old Cheeseman reading there by himself. He was always as mild as the tea—and *that's* pretty mild, I should hope!—so when they whistled to him, he looked up and nodded; and when they said, "Halloa, Old Cheeseman, what have you had for dinner?" he said, "Boiled mutton"; and when they said, "An't it solitary, Old Cheeseman?" he said, "It is a little dull sometimes": and then they said, "Well, good-bye, Old Cheeseman!" and climbed down again. Of course it was imposing on Old Cheeseman to give him nothing but boiled mutton through a whole Vacation, but that was just like the system. When they didn't give him boiled mutton, they gave him rice pudding, pretending it was a treat. And saved the butcher.

So Old Cheeseman went on. The holidays brought him into other trouble besides the loneliness; because when the fellows began to come back, not wanting to, he was always glad to see them; which was aggravating when they were not at all glad to see him, and so he got his head knocked against walls, and that was the way his nose bled. But he was a favourite in general. Once a subscription was raised for him; and, to keep up his spirits, he was presented before the holidays with two white mice, a rabbit, a pigeon, and a beautiful puppy. Old Cheeseman cried about it—especially soon afterwards, when they all ate one another.

Of course Old Cheeseman used to be called by the names of all sorts of cheeses—Double Glo'sterman, Family Cheshireman, Dutchman, North Wiltshireman, and all that. But he never minded it. And I don't mean to say he was old in point of years—because he wasn't—only he was called from the first, Old Cheeseman.

At last, Old Cheeseman was made second Latin Master.

He was brought in one morning at the beginning of a new half, and presented to the school in that capacity as "Mr. Cheeseman." Then our fellows all agreed that Old Cheeseman was a spy, and a deserter, who had gone over to the enemy's camp, and sold himself for gold. It was no excuse for him that he had sold himself for very little gold —two pound ten a quarter and his washing, as was reported. It was decided by a Parliament which sat about it, that Old Cheeseman's mercenary motives could alone be taken into account, and that he had "coined our blood for drachmas." The Parliament took the expression out of the quarrel scene between Brutus and Cassius.

When it was settled in this strong way that Old Cheeseman was a tremendous traitor, who had wormed himself into our fellows' secrets on purpose to get himself into favor by giving up everything he knew, all courageous fellows were invited to come forward and enroll themselves in a Society for making a set against him. The President of the Society was First Boy, named Bob Tarter. His father was in the West Indies, and he owned, himself, that his father was worth Millions. He had great power among our fellows, and he wrote a parody, beginning—

> "Who made believe to be so meek
>   That we could hardly hear him speak,
>   Yet turned out an Informing Sneak?
>   Old Cheeseman."

—and on in that way through more than a dozen verses, which he used to go and sing, every morning, close by the new master's desk. He trained one of the low boys, too, a rosy-cheeked little Brass who didn't care what he did, to go up to him with his Latin Grammar one morning, and say it so; *Nominativus pronominum*—Old Cheeseman, *raro exprimitur*—was never suspected, *nisi distinctionis*—of being an informer, *aut emphasis gratia*—until he proved one. *Ut*—for instance, *Vos damnastis*—when he sold the boys. *Quasi*—as though, *dicat*—he should say, *Pretaerea nemo*—I'm a Judas! All this produced a great effect on Old Cheeseman. He had never had much hair; but what he had, began to get thinner and thinner every day. He grew paler and more worn; and sometimes of an evening he was seen sitting at his desk with a precious long snuff to his candle, and his hands before his face, crying. But no member of the Society could pity him, even if he felt inclined, because the President said it was Old Cheeseman's conscience.

So Old Cheeseman went on, and didn't he lead a miserable life! Of course the Reverend turned up his nose at him, and of course *she* did—because both of them always do that at all the masters—but he suffered from the fellows most, and he suffered from them constantly. He never told about it, that the Society could find out; but he got no credit for that, because the President said it was Old Cheeseman's cowardice.

He had only one friend in the world, and that one was almost as powerless as he was, for it was only Jane. Jane was a sort of wardrobe woman to our fellows, and took care of the boxes. She had come at first, I believe, as a kind of apprentice—some of our fellows say from a Charity, but *I* don't know—and after her time was out, had stopped at so much a year. So little a year, perhaps I ought to say, for it is far more likely. However, she had put some pounds in the Savings' Bank, and she was a very nice young woman. She was not quite pretty; but she had a very frank, honest, bright face, and all our fellows were fond of her. She was uncommonly neat and cheerful, and uncommonly comfortable and kind. And if anything was the matter with a fellow's mother, he always went and showed the letter to Jane.

Jane was Old Cheeseman's friend. The more the Society went against him, the more Jane stood by him. She used to give him a good-humored look out of her still-room window, sometimes, that seemed to set him up for the day. She used to pass out of the orchard and the kitchen garden (always kept locked, I believe you!) through the playground, when she might have gone the other way, only to give a turn of her head, as much as to say "Keep up your spirits!" to Old Cheeseman. His slip of a room was so fresh and orderly that it was well known who looked after it while he was at his desk; and when our fellows saw a smoking hot dumpling on his plate at dinner, they knew with indignation who had sent it up.

Under these circumstances, the Society resolved, after a quantity of meeting and debating, that Jane should be requested to cut Old Cheeseman dead; and that if she refused, she must be sent to Coventry herself. So a deputation, headed by the President, was appointed to wait on Jane, and inform her of the vote the Society had been under the painful necessity of passing. She was very much respected for all her good qualities, and there was a story about her having once waylaid the Reverend in his own study, and got a fellow off from severe punishment, of her own kind comfortable heart. So the deputation didn't much like the job. However, they went up, and the President told Jane all about it. Upon which Jane turned very red, burst into tears, informed the President and the deputation, in a way not at all like her usual way, that they were a parcel of malicious young savages, and turned the whole respected body out of the room. Consequently it was entered in the Society's book (kept in astronomical cypher for fear of detection), that all communication with Jane was interdicted: and the President addressed the members on this convincing instance of Old Cheeseman's undermining.

But Jane was as true to Old Cheeseman as Old Cheeseman was false to our fellows—in their opinion, at all events—and steadily continued to be his only friend. It was a great exasperation to the Society, because Jane was as much a loss to them as she was a gain to him; and being more inveterate against him than ever, they treated him worse than ever. At last, one morning, his desk stood empty, his room was peeped into, and found to be vacant, and a whisper went about among the pale faces of our fellows that Old Cheeseman, unable to bear it any longer, had got up early and drowned himself.

The mysterious looks of the other masters after breakfast, and the evident fact that Old Cheeseman was not expected confirmed the Society in this opinion. Some began to discuss whether the President was liable to hanging or only transportation for life, and the President's face

showed a great anxiety to know which. However, he said
that a jury of his country should find him game; and that
in his address he should put it to them to lay their hands
upon their hearts and say whether they as Britons approved of informers, and how they thought they would
like it themselves. Some of the Society considered that he
had better run away until he found a forest where he
might change clothes with a woodcutter, and stain his
face with blackberries; but the majority believed that if he
stood his ground, his father—belonging as he did to the
West Indies, and being worth millions—could buy him
off.

All our fellows' hearts beat fast when the Reverend
came in, and made a sort of a Roman, or a Field Marshal,
of himself with the ruler; as he always did before deliver-
ing an address. But their fears were nothing to their aston-
ishment when he came out with the story that Old Cheeseman, "so long our respected friend and fellow-pilgrim in
the pleasant plains of knowledge," he called him—O yes!
I dare say! Much of that!—was the orphan child of a
disinherited young lady who had married against her father's wish, and whose young husband had died, and who
died of sorrow herself, and whose unfortunate baby (Old
Cheeseman) had been brought up at the cost of a grandfather who would never consent to see it, baby, boy, or man:
which grandfather was now dead, and serve him right—
that's *my* putting in—and which grandfather's large property, there being no will, was now, and all of a sudden and
for ever, Old Cheeseman's! Our so long respected friend
and fellow-pilgrim in the pleasant plains of knowledge,

the Reverend wound up a lot of bothering quotations by saying, would "come among us once more" that day fortnight when he desired to take leave of us himself, in a more particular manner. With these words, he stared severely round at our fellows, and went solemnly out.

There was precious consternation among the members of the Society, now. Lots of them wanted to resign, and lots more began to try to make out that they had never belonged to it. However, the President stuck up, and said that they must stand or fall together, and that if a breach was made it should be over his body—which was meant to encourage the Society: but it didn't. The President further said, he would consider the position in which they stood, and would give them his best opinion and advice in a few days. This was eagerly looked for, as he knew a good deal of the world on account of his father's being in the West Indies.

After days and days of hard thinking, and drawing armies all over his slate, the President called our fellows together and made the matter clear. He said it was plain that when Old Cheeseman came on the appointed day, his first revenge would be to impeach the Society, and have it flogged all round. After witnessing with joy the torture of his enemies, and gloating over the cries which agony would extort from them, the probability was that he would invite the Reverend, on pretense of conversation, into a private room—say the parlor into which Parents were shown, where the two great globes were which were never used—and would there reproach him with the various frauds and oppressions he had endured at his hands.

At the close of his observations he would make a signal to a Prizefighter concealed in the passage, who would then appear and pitch into the Reverend, till he was left insensible. Old Cheeseman would then make Jane a present of from five to ten pounds, and would leave the establishment in fiendish triumph.

The President explained that against the parlor part, or the Jane part, of these arrangements he had nothing to say; but, on the part of the Society, he counseled deadly resistance. With this view he recommended that all available desks should be filled with stones, and that the first word of the complaint should be the signal to every fellow to let fly at Old Cheeseman. The bold advice put the Society in better spirits, and was unanimously taken. A post about Old Cheeseman's size was put up in the playground, and all our fellows practiced at it till it was dinted all over.

When the day came, and Places were called, every fellow sat down in a tremble. There had been much discussing and disputing as to how Old Cheeseman would come; but it was the general opinion that he would appear in a sort of triumphal car drawn by four horses, with two livery servants in front, and the Prizefighter in disguise up behind. So, all our fellows sat listening for the sound of wheels. But no wheels were heard, for Old Cheeseman walked after all, and came into the school without any preparation. Pretty much as he used to be, only dressed in black.

"Gentlemen," said the Reverend, presenting him, "our so long respected friend and fellow-pilgrim in the pleasant plains of knowledge, is desirous to offer a word or two. Attention, gentlemen, one and all!"

Every fellow stole his hand into his desk and looked at the President. The President was all ready, and taking aim at Old Cheeseman with his eyes.

What did Old Cheeseman then, but walk up to his old desk, look round him with a queer smile as if there was a tear in his eye, and begin in a quavering, mild voice, "My dear companions and old friends!"

Every fellow's hand came out of his desk, and the President suddenly began to cry.

"My dear companions and old friends," said Old Cheeseman, "you have heard of my good fortune. I have passed so many years under this roof—my entire life so far, I may say—that I hope you have been glad to hear of it for my sake. I could never enjoy it without exchanging congratulations with you. If we have ever misunderstood one another at all, pray, my dear boys, let us forgive and forget. I have a great tenderness for you, and I am sure you return it. I want in the fulness of a grateful heart to shake hands with you every one. I have come back to do it, if you please, my dear boys."

Since the President had begun to cry, several other fellows had broken out here and there: but now, when Old Cheeseman began with him as first boy, laid his left hand affectionately on his shoulder and gave him his right; and when the President said "Indeed, I don't deserve it, sir; upon my honor I don't;" there was sobbing and crying all over the school. Every other fellow said he didn't deserve it, much in the same way; but Old Cheeseman, not minding that a bit, went cheerfully round to every boy, and wound up with every master—finishing off the Reverend last.

Then a sniveling little chap in a corner, who was always under some punishment or other, set up a shrill cry of "Success to Old Cheeseman! Hooray!" The Reverend glared upon him, and said, *"Mr.* Cheeseman, sir." But, Old Cheeseman protesting that he liked his old name a great deal better than his new one, all our fellows took up the cry; and, for I don't know how many minutes, there was such a thundering of feet and hands, and such a roaring of Old Cheeseman, as never was heard.

After that, there was a spread in the dining-room of the most magnificent kind. Fowls, tongues, preserves, fruits, confectionaries, jellies, neguses, barley-sugar temples, trifles, crackers—eat all you can and pocket what you like—all at Old Cheeseman's expense. After that, speeches, whole holiday, double and treble sets of all manners of things for all manners of games, donkeys, pony-chaises and drive yourself, dinner for all the masters at the Seven Bells (twenty pounds a-head our fellows estimated it at), an annual holiday and feast fixed for that day every year, and another on Old Cheeseman's birthday—Reverend bound down before the fellows to allow it, so that he could never back out—all at Old Cheeseman's expense.

And didn't our fellows go down in a body and cheer outside the Seven Bells? O no!

But there's something else besides. Don't look at the next storyteller, for there's more yet. Next day, it was resolved that the Society should make it up with Jane, and then be dissolved. What do you thing of Jane being gone, though! "What? Gone for ever?" said our fellows, with long faces. "Yes, to be sure," was all the answer they could get. None of the people about the house would say anything more. At length, the first boy took upon himself to ask the Reverend whether our old friend Jane was really gone? The Reverend (he has got a daughter at home —turn-up nose, and red) replied severely, "Yes, sir, Miss Pitt is gone." The idea of calling Jane, Miss Pitt! Some said she had been sent away in disgrace for taking money from Old Cheeseman; others said she had gone into Old Cheeseman's service at a rise of ten pounds a year. All that our fellows knew, was, she was gone.

It was two or three months afterwards, when, one afternoon, an open carriage stopped at the cricket field, just outside bounds, with a lady and gentleman in it, who looked at the game a long time and stood up to see it played. Nobody thought much about them, until the same little sniveling chap came in, against all rules, from the post where he was Scout, and said, "It's Jane!" Both Elevens forgot the game directly, and ran crowding round the carriage. It *was* Jane! In such a bonnet! And if you'll believe me, Jane was married to Old Cheeseman.

It soon became quite a regular thing when our fellows were hard at it in the playground, to see a carriage at the low part of the wall where it joins the high part, and a lady and gentleman standing up in it, looking over. The gentleman was always Old Cheeseman, and the lady was always Jane.

The first time I ever saw them, I saw them in that way.

There had been a good many changes among our fellows then, and it had turned out that Bob Tarter's father wasn't worth Millions! He wasn't worth anything. Bob had gone for a soldier, and Old Cheeseman had purchased his discharge. But that's not the carriage. The carriage stopped, and all our fellows stopped as soon as it was seen.

"So you have never sent me to Coventry after all!" said the lady, laughing, as our fellows swarmed up to the wall to shake hands with her. "Are you never going to do it?"

"Never! never! never!" on all sides.

I didn't understand what she meant then, but of course I do now. I was very much pleased with her face though, and with her good way, and I couldn't help looking at her —and at him too—with all our fellows clustering so joyfully about them.

They soon took notice of me as a new boy, so I thought I might as well swarm up the wall myself, and shake hands with them as the rest did. I was quite as glad to see them as the rest were, and was quite as familiar with them in a moment.

"Only a fortnight now," said Old Cheeseman, "to the holidays. Who stops? Anybody?"

A good many fingers pointed at me, and a good many voices cried "He does!" For it was the year when you were all away; and rather low I was about it, I can tell you.

"Oh!" said Old Cheeseman. "But it's solitary here in the holiday time. He had better come to us."

So I went to their delightful house and was as happy as I could possibly be. They understand how to conduct themselves towards boys, *they* do. When they take a boy to the play for instance, they *do* take him. They don't go in after it's begun, or come out before it's over. They know how to bring a boy up, too. Look at their own! Though he is very little as yet, what a capital boy he is! Why, my next favorite to Mrs. Cheeseman and Old Cheeseman, is young Cheeseman.

So, now I have told you all I know about Old Cheeseman. And it's not much after all I am afraid. Is it?

Nobody's Story

He lived on the bank of a mighty river, broad and deep, which was always silently rolling on to a vast undiscovered ocean. It had rolled on, ever since the world began. It had changed its course sometimes, and turned into new channels, leaving its old ways dry and barren; but it had ever been upon the flow, and ever was to flow until time should be no more. Against its strong, unfathomable stream, nothing made head. No living creature, no flower, no leaf, no particle of animate or inanimate existence, ever strayed back from the undiscovered ocean. The tide of the river set resistlessly towards it; and the tide never stopped, any more than the earth stops in its circling round the sun.

He lived in a busy place, and he worked very hard to live. He had no hope of ever being rich enough to live a month without hard work, but he was quite content, GOD knows, to labor with a cheerful will. He was one of an immense family, all of whose sons and daughters gained

their daily bread by daily work, prolonged from their rising up betimes until their lying down at night. Beyond
this destiny he had no prospect, and he sought none.

There was over-much drumming, trumpeting, and
speech-making, in the neighborhood where he dwelt; but
he had nothing to do with that. Such clash and uproar
came from the Bigwig family, at the unaccountable pro-
ceedings of which race, he marveled much. They set up
the strangest statues, in iron, marble, bronze, and brass,
before his door; and darkened his house with the legs and
tails of uncouth images of horses. He wondered what it all
meant, smiled in a rough good-humored way he had, and
kept at his hard work.

The Bigwig family (composed of all the stateliest people thereabouts, and all the noisiest) had undertaken to
save him the trouble of thinking for himself, and to manage him and his affairs. "Why truly," said he, "I have
little time upon my hands; and if you will be so good as to
take care of me, in return for the money I pay over"—for
the Bigwig family were not above his money—"I shall be
relieved and much obliged, considering that you know
best." Hence the drumming, trumpeting, and speechmak-
ing, and the ugly images of horses which he was expected
to fall down and worship.

"I don't understand all this," said he, rubbing his fur-
rowed brow confusedly. "But it *has* a meaning, maybe, if I
could find it out."

"It means," returned the Bigwig family, suspecting
something of what he said, "honor and glory in the highest, to the highest merit."

"Oh!" said he. And he was glad to hear that.

But, when he looked among the images in iron, marble, bronze, and brass, he failed to find a rather meritorious countryman of his, once the son of a Warwickshire wool-dealer, or any single countryman whomsoever of that kind. He could find none of the men whose knowledge had rescued him and his children from terrific and disfiguring disease, whose boldness had raised his forefathers from the condition of serfs, whose wise fancy had opened a new and high existence to the humblest, whose skill had filled the working man's world with accumulated wonders. Whereas, he did find others whom he knew no good of, and even others whom he knew much ill of.

"Humph!" said he. "I don't quite understand it."

So, he went home, and sat down by his fireside to get it out of his mind.

Now, his fireside was a bare one, all hemmed in by blackened streets; but it was a precious place to him. The hands of his wife were hardened with toil, and she was old before her time; but she was dear to him. His children, stunted in their growth, bore traces of unwholesome nurture; but they had beauty in his sight. Above all other things, it was an earnest desire of this man's soul that his children should be taught. "If I am sometimes misled," said he, "for want of knowledge, at least let them know better, and avoid my mistakes. If it is hard to me to reap the harvest of pleasure and instruction that is stored in books, let it be easier to them."

But, the Bigwig family broke out into violent family quarrels concerning what it was lawful to teach to this

man's children. Some of the family insisted on such a
thing being primary and indispensable above all other
things; and other of the family insisted on such another
thing being primary and indispensable above all other
things; and the Bigwig family, rent into factions, wrote
pamphlets, held convocations, delivered charges, orations,
and all varieties of discourses; impounded one another in
courts Lay and courts Ecclesiastical; threw dirt, ex-
changed pummelings, and fell together by the ears in
unintelligible animosity. Meanwhile, this man, in his short
evening snatches at his fireside, saw the demon Ignorance
arise there, and take his children to itself. He saw his
daughter perverted into a heavy, slatternly drudge; he
saw his son go moping down the ways of low sensuality,
to brutality and crime; he saw the dawning light of intelligence in the eyes of his babies so changing into cunning
and suspicion, that he could have rather wished them
idiots.

"I don't understand this any the better," said he; "but I
think it cannot be right. Nay, by the clouded Heaven
above me, I protest against this as my wrong!"

Becoming peaceable again (for his passion was usually
shortlived, and his nature kind), he looked about him on
his Sundays and holidays, and he saw how much monot-
ony and weariness there was, and thence how drunkenness
arose with all its train of ruin. Then he appealed to the
Bigwig family, and said, "We are a laboring people, and I
have a glimmering suspicion in me that laboring people of
whatever condition were made—by a higher intelligence
than yours, as I poorly understand it—to be in need of

mental refreshment and recreation. See what we fall into, when we rest without it. Come! Amuse me harmlessly, show me something, give me an escape!"

But, here the Bigwig family fell into a state of uproar absolutely deafening. When some few voices were faintly heard, proposing to show him the wonders of the world, the greatness of creation, the mighty changes of time, the workings of nature and the beauties of art—to show him these things, that is to say, at any period of his life when he could look upon them—there arose among the Bigwigs such roaring and raving, such pulpiting and petitioning, such maundering and memorializing, such name-calling and dirt-throwing, such a shrill wind of parliamentary questioning and feeble replying—where "I dare not" waited on "I would"—that the poor fellow stood aghast, staring wildly around.

"Have I provoked all this," said he, with his hands to his affrighted ears, "by what was meant to be an innocent request, plainly arising out of my familiar experience, and the common knowledge of all men who choose to open their eyes? I don't understand, and I am not understood. What is to come of such a state of things!"

He was bending over his work, often asking himself the question, when the news began to spread that a pestilence had appeared among the laborers, and was slaying them by thousands. Going forth to look about him, he soon found this to be true. The dying and the dead were mingled in the close and tainted houses among which his life was passed. New poison was distilled into the always murky, always sickening air. The robust and the weak, old age and infancy, the father and the mother, all were stricken down alike.

What means of flight had he? He remained there, where he was, and saw those who were dearest to him die. A kind preacher came to him, and would have said some prayers to soften his heart in his gloom, but he replied:

"O what avails it, missionary, to come to me, a man condemned to residence in this faetid place, where every sense bestowed upon me for my delight becomes a torment, and where every minute of my numbered days is new mire added to the heap under which I lie oppressed! But, give me my first glimpse of Heaven, through a little of its light and air; give me pure water; help me to be clean; lighten this heavy atmosphere and heavy life, in which our spirits sink, and we become the indifferent and callous creatures you too often see us; gently and kindly take the bodies of those who die among us, out of the small room where we grow to be so familiar with the awful change that even ITS sanctity is lost to us; and, Teacher, then I will hear—none know better than you, how willingly—of Him whose thoughts were so much with the poor, and who had compassion for all human sorrow!"

He was at work again, solitary and sad, when his Master came and stood near to him dressed in black. He, also, had suffered heavily. His young wife, his beautiful and good young wife, was dead; so, too, his only child.

"Master, 'tis hard to bear—I know it—but be comforted. I would give you comfort, if I could."

The Master thanked him from his heart, but, said he, "O you laboring men! The calamity began among you. If you had but lived more healthily and decently, I should not be the widowed and bereft mourner that I am this day."

"Master," returned the other, shaking his head, "I have begun to understand a little that most calamities will come from us, as this one did, and that none will stop at our poor doors, until we are united with that great squabbling family yonder, to do the things that are right. We cannot live healthily and decently, unless they who undertook to manage us provide the means. We cannot be instructed unless they will teach us; we cannot be rationally amused, unless they will amuse us; we cannot but have some false gods of our own, while they set up so many of theirs in all the public places. The evil consequences of imperfect instruction, the evil consequences of pernicious neglect, the evil consequences of unnatural restraint and the denial of humanizing enjoyments, will all come from us, and none of them will stop with us. They will spread far and wide. They always do; they always have done—just like the pestilence. I understand so much, I think, at last."

But the Master said again, "O you laboring men! How seldom do we ever hear of you, except in connection with some trouble!"

"Master," he replied, "I am Nobody, and little likely

to be heard of (nor yet much wanted to be heard of, perhaps), except when there *is* some trouble. But it never
begins with me, and it never can end with me. As sure as
Death, it comes down to me and it goes up from me."

There was so much reason in what he said, that the
Bigwig family, getting wind of it, and being horribly
frightened by the late desolation, resolved to unite with
him to do the things that were right—at all events, so far
as the said things were associated with the direct preven-
tion, humanly speaking, of another pestilence. But, as
their fear wore off, which it soon began to do, they resumed their falling out among themselves, and did nothing. Consequently the scourge appeared again—low down
as before—and spread avengingly upward as before, and
carried off vast numbers of the brawlers. But not a man
among them ever admitted, if in the least degree he ever
perceived, that he had anything to do with it.

So Nobody lived and died in the old, old, old way; and
this, in the main, is the whole of Nobody's story.

Had he no name, you ask? Perhaps it was Legion. It
matters little what his name was. Let us call him Legion.

If you were ever in the Belgian villages near the field of
Waterloo, you will have seen, in some quiet little church,
a monument erected by faithful companions in arms to the
memory of Colonel A, Major B, Captains C, D and E,
Lieutenants F and G, Ensigns H, I and J, seven non-commissioned officers, and one hundred and thirty rank and
file, who fell in the discharge of their duty on the memorable day. The story of Nobody is the story of the rank and
file of the earth. They bear their share of the battle; they

have their part in the victory; they fall; they leave no name but in the mass. The march of the proudest of us, leads to the dusty way by which they go. O! Let us think of them this year at the Christmas fire, and not forget them when it is burnt out.

THE SEVEN POOR TRAVELLERS

CHAPTER I
In the Old City of Rochester

trictly speaking, there were only six Poor Travellers; but, being a Traveller myself, though an idle one, and being withal as poor as I hope to be, I brought the number up to seven. This word of explanation is due at once, for what says the inscription over the quaint old door?

RICHARD WATTS, ESQ.
by his Will, dated 22 Aug. 1579,
founded this Charity
for Six poor Travellers,
who not being ROGUES, or PROCTORS,
May receive gratis for one Night,
Lodging, Entertainment,
and Fourpence each.

It was in the ancient little city of Rochester in Kent, of all the good days in the year upon a Christmas-eve, that I stood reading this inscription over the quaint old door in question. I had been wandering about the neighboring Cathedral, and had seen the tomb of Richard Watts, with the effigy of worthy Master Richard starting out of it like a ship's figurehead; and I had felt that I could do no less, as I gave the Verger his fee, than inquire the way to Watts's Charity. The way being very short and very plain, I had come prosperously to the inscription and the quaint old door.

"Now," said I to myself, as I looked at the knocker, "I know I am not a Proctor; I wonder whether I am a Rogue!"

Upon the whole, though Conscience reproduced two or three pretty faces which might have had smaller attraction for a moral Goliath than they had had for me, who am but a Tom Thumb in that way, came to the conclusion that I was not a Rogue. So, beginning to regard the establishment as in some sort my property, bequeathed to me and divers co-legatees, share and share alike, by the Worshipful Master Richard Watts, I stepped backward into the road to survey my inheritance.

I found it to be a clean white house, of a staid and venerable air, with the quaint old door already three times mentioned (an arched door), choice, little, long, low lattice-windows, and a roof of three gables. The silent High Street of Rochester is full of gables, with old beams and timbers carved into strange faces. It is oddly garnished with a queer old clock that projects over the pavement out of a grave red-brick building, as if Time carried on business there, and hung out his sign. Sooth to say, he did an

active stroke of work in Rochester, in the old days of the
Romans, and the Saxons, and the Normans; and down to
the times of King John, when the rugged castle—I will
not undertake to say how many hundreds of years old then
—was abandoned to the centuries of weather which have
so defaced the dark apertures in its walls, that the ruin
looks as if the rocks and daws had pecked its eyes out.

I was very well pleased, both with my property and its
situation. While I was yet surveying it with growing content, I spied at one of the upper lattices which stood open,
a decent body, of a wholesome matronly appearance,
whose eyes I caught inquiringly addressed to mine. They
said so plainly, "Do you wish to see the house?" that I
answered aloud, "Yes, if you please." And within a minute the old door opened, and I bent my head, and went
down two steps into the entry.

"This," said the matronly presence, ushering me into a
low room on the right, "is where the travellers sit by the
fire, and cook what bits of suppers they buy with their
fourpences."

"O! Then they have no Entertainment?" said I. For the
inscription over the outer door was still running in my
head, and I was mentally repeating, in a kind of tune,
"Lodging, entertainment, and fourpence each."

"They have a fire provided for 'em," returned the matron, —a mighty civil person, not, as I could make out,
overpaid; "and these cooking utensils. And this what's
painted on a board is the rules for their behavior. They
have their fourpences when they get their tickets from the
steward over the way, —for I don't admit 'em myself,

they must get their tickets first, and sometimes one buys a rasher of bacon, and another a herring, and another a pound of potatoes, or what not. Sometimes two or three of 'em will club their fourpences together, and make a supper that way. But not much of anything is to be got for fourpence, at present, when provisions is so dear."

"True indeed," I remarked. I had been looking about the room, admiring its snug fireside at the upper end, its glimpse of the street through the low mullioned window, and its beams overhead. "It is very comfortable," said I.

"Ill-conwenient," observed the matronly presence.

I liked to hear her say so; for it showed a commendable anxiety to execute in no niggardly spirit the intentions of Master Richard Watts. But the room was really so well adapted to its purpose that I protested, quite enthusiastically, against her disparagement.

"Nay, ma'am," said I, "I am sure it is warm in winter and cool in summer. It has a look of homely welcome and soothing rest. It has a remarkably cozy fireside, the very blink of which, gleaming out into the street upon a winter night, is enough to warm all Rochester's heart. And as to the convenience of the six Poor Travellers—"

"I don't mean them," returned the presence. "I speak of its being an ill-conwenience to myself and my daughter, having no other room to sit in of a night."

This was true enough, but there was another quaint room of corresponding dimensions on the opposite side of the entry: so I stepped across to it, through the open doors of both rooms, and asked what this chamber was for.

"This," returned the presence, "is the Board Room. Where the gentlemen meet when they come here."

Let me see. I had counted from the street six upper windows besides these on the ground-story. Making a perplexed calculation in my mind, I rejoined, "Then the six Poor Travellers sleep upstairs?"

My new friend shook her head. "They sleep," she answered, "in two little outer galleries at the back, where their beds has always been, ever since the Charity was founded. It being so very ill-conwenient to me as things is at present, the gentlemen are going to take off a bit of the back yard, and make a slip of a room for 'em there, to sit in before they go to bed."

"And then the six Poor Travellers," said I, "will be entirely out of the house?"

"Entirely out of the house," assented the presence, comfortably smoothing her hands. "Which is considered much better for all parties, and much more conwenient."

I had been a little startled, in the Cathedral, by the emphasis with which the effigy of Master Richard Watts was bursting out of his tomb; but I began to think, now, that it might be expected to come across the High Street some stormy night, and make a disturbance here.

Howbeit, I kept my thoughts to myself, and accompanied the presence to the little galleries at the back. I found them on a tiny scale, like the galleries in old inn-yards; and they were very clean. While I was looking at them, the matron gave me to understand that the prescribed number of Poor Travellers were forthcoming every night from year's end to year's end; and that the beds were always occupied. My questions upon this, and her replies, brought us back to the Board Room so essential to the dignity of "the gentlemen," where she showed me the printed accounts of the Charity hanging up by the window. From them I gathered that the greater part of the property bequeathed by the Worshipful Master Richard Watts for the maintenance of this foundation was, at the period of his death, mere marshland; but that, in course of time, it had been reclaimed and built upon, and was very considerably increased in value. I found, too, that about a thirtieth part of the annual revenue was now expended on the purposes commemorated in the inscription over the door; the rest being handsomely laid out in Chancery, law expenses, collectorship, receivership, poundage, and other appendages of management, highly complimentary to the importance of the six Poor Travellers. In short, I made the not entirely new discovery that it may be said of an establishment like this, in dear old England, as of the fat oyster in the American story, that it takes a good many men to swallow it whole.

"And pray, ma'am," said I, sensible that the blankness of my face began to brighten as the thought occurred to me, "could one see these Travellers?"

"Well!" she returned dubiously, "no!"

"Not tonight, for instance!" said I.

"Well!" she returned more positively, "no. Nobody ever asked to see them, and nobody ever did see them."

As I am not easily baulked in a design when I am set upon it, I urged to the good lady that this was Christmas-eve; that Christmas comes but once a year, —which is unhappily too true, for when it begins to stay with us the whole year round we shall make this earth a very different place; that I was possessed by the desire to treat the Travellers to a supper and a temperate glass of hot Wassail; that the voice of Fame had been heard in that land, declaring my ability to make hot Wassail; that if I were permitted to hold the feast, I should be found conformable to reason, sobriety, and good hours; in a word, that I could be merry and wise myself, and had been even known at a pinch to keep others so, although I was decorated with no badge or medal, and was not a Brother, Orator, Apostle, Saint, or Prophet of any denomination whatever. In the end I prevailed, to my great joy. It was settled that at nine o'clock that night a Turkey and a piece of Roast Beef should smoke upon the board; and that I, faint and unworthy minister for once of Master Richard Watts, should preside as the Christmas-supper host of the six Poor Travellers.

I went back to my inn to give the necessary directions for the Turkey and Roast Beef, and, during the remainder of the day, could settle to nothing for thinking of the Poor Travellers. When the wind blew hard against the windows,—it was a cold day, with dark gusts of sleet alternating with periods of wild brightness, as if the year were dying fitfully, —I pictured them advancing towards their resting-place along various cold roads, and felt delighted to think how little they foresaw the supper that awaited them. I painted their portraits in my mind, and indulged in little heightening touches. I made them footsore; I made them weary; I made them carry packs and bundles; I made

them stop by finger-posts and milestones, leaning on their
bent sticks, and looking wistfully at what was written
there; I made them lose their way; and filled their five wits
with apprehensions of lying out all night, and being frozen
to death. I took up my hat, and went out, climbed to the
top of the Old Castle, and looked over the windy hills that
slope down to the Medway, almost believing that I could
descry some of my Travellers in the distance. After it fell
dark, and the Cathedral bell was heard in the invisible
steeple—quite a bower of frosty rime when I had last seen
it—striking five, six, seven, I became so full of my Travellers that I could eat no dinner, and felt constrained to
watch them still in the red coals of my fire. They were all
arrived by this time, I thought, had got their tickets, and
were gone in. —There my pleasure was dashed by the
reflection that probably some Travellers had come too late
and were shut out.

After the Cathedral bell had struck eight, I could smell
a delicious savor of Turkey and Roast Beef rising to the
window of my adjoining bedroom, which looked down
into the inn-yard just where the lights of the kitchen red-
dened a massive fragment of the Castle Wall. It was high
time to make the Wassail now; therefore I had up the
materials (which, together with their proportions and
combinations, I must decline to impart, as the only secret
of my own I was ever known to keep), and made a glorious jorum. Not in a bowl; for a bowl anywhere but on a
shelf is a low superstition, fraught with cooling and slop-
ping; but in a brown earthenware pitcher, tenderly suffo-
cated, when full, with a coarse cloth. It being now upon

the stroke of nine, I set out for Watts's Charity, carrying my brown beauty in my arms. I would trust Ben, the waiter, with untold gold; but there are strings in the human heart which must never be sounded by another, and drinks that I make myself are those strings in mine.

The Travellers were all assembled, the cloth was laid, and Ben brought a great billet of wood, and had laid it artfully on the top of the fire, so that a touch or two of the poker after supper should make a roaring blaze. Having deposited my brown beauty in a red nook of the hearth, inside the fender, where she soon began to sing like an ethereal cricket, diffusing at the same time odors as of ripe vineyards, spice forests, and orange groves, —I say, having stationed my beauty in a place of security and improvement, I introduced myself to my guests by shaking hands all round, and giving them a hearty welcome.

I found the party to be thus composed. Firstly, myself. Secondly, a very decent man indeed, with his right arm in a sling, who had a certain clean, agreeable smell of wood about him, from which I judged him to have something to do with shipbuilding. Thirdly, a little sailor-boy, a mere child, with a profusion of rich dark brown hair, and deep womanly-looking eyes. Fourthly, a shabby-genteel personage in a threadbare black suit, and apparently in very bad circumstances, with a dry, suspicious look; the absent buttons on his waistcoat eked out with red tape; and a bundle of extraordinarily tattered papers sticking out of an inner breast-pocket. Fifthly, a foreigner by birth, but an Englishman in speech, who carried his pipe in the band of his hat, and lost no time in telling me, in an easy, simple, engaging way, that he was a watchmaker from Geneva, and travelled all about the Continent, mostly on foot, working as a journeyman, and seeing new countries, —possibly (I thought) also smuggling a watch or so, now and then. Sixthly, a little widow, who had been very pretty and was still very young, but whose beauty had been wrecked in some great misfortune, and whose manner was remarkably timid, scared, and solitary. Seventhly and lastly, a Traveller of a kind familiar to my boyhood, but now almost obsolete, —a Book-Peddler, who had a quantity of Pamphlets and Numbers with him, and who presently boasted that he could repeat more verses in an evening than he could sell in a twelvemonth.

All these I have mentioned in the order in which they sat at table. I presided, and the matronly presence faced me. We were not long in taking our places, for the supper had arrived with me, in the following procession:

Myself with the pitcher.

Ben with Beer.

Inattentive Boy with hot plates. Inattentive Boy

with hot plates.

THE TURKEY.

Female carrying sauces to be heated on the spot.

THE BEEF.

Man with Tray on his head, containing Vegetables

and Sundries.

Volunteer Hostler from Hotel, grinning,

And rendering no assistance.

As we passed along the High Street, comet-like, we left a long tail of fragrance behind us which caused the public to stop, sniffing in wonder. We had previously left at the corner of the inn-yard a wall-eyed young man connected with the Fly department, and well accustomed to the sound of a railway whistle which Ben always carries in his pocket, whose instructions were, so soon as he should hear the whistle blown, to dash into the kitchen, seize the hot plum-pudding and mince-pies, and speed with them to Watts's Charity, where they would be received (he was further instructed) by the sauce-female, who would be provided with brandy in a blue state of combustion.

All these arrangements were executed in the most exact and punctual manner. I never saw a finer turkey, finer beef, or greater prodigality of sauce and gravy; and my Travellers did wonderful justice to everything set before them. It made my heart rejoice to observe how their wind and frost hardened faces softened in the clatter of plates and knives and forks, and mellowed in the fire and supper heat. While their hats and caps and wrappers, hanging up, a few small bundles on the ground in a corner, and in another corner three or four old walking-sticks, worn down at the end to mere fringe, linked this snug interior with the bleak outside in a golden chain.

When supper was done, and my brown beauty had been elevated on the table, there was a general requisition to me to "take the corner"; which suggested to me comfortably enough how much my friends here made of a fire, —for when had *I* ever thought so highly of the corner, since the days when I connected it with Jack Horner? However, as

I declined, Ben, whose touch on all convivial instruments is perfect, drew the table apart, and instructing my Travellers to open right and left on either side of me, and form round the fire, closed up the center with myself and my chair, and preserved the order we had kept at table. He had already, in a tranquil manner, boxed the ears of the inattentive boys until they had been by imperceptible degrees boxed out of the room; and he now rapidly skirmished the sauce-female into the High Street, disappeared, and softly closed the door.

This was the time for bringing the poker to bear on the billet of wood. I tapped it three times, like an enchanted talisman, and a brilliant host of merry-makers burst out of it, and sported off by the chimney, —rushing up the middle in a fiery country dance, and never coming down again. Meanwhile, by their sparkling light, which threw our lamp into the shade, I filled the glasses, and gave my Travellers, CHRISTMAS! —CHRISTMAS-EVE, my friends, when the shepherds, who were Poor Travellers, too, in their way, heard the Angels sing, "On earth, peace. Goodwill towards men!"

I don't know who was the first among us to think that we ought to take hands as we sat, in deference to the toast, or whether any one of us anticipated the others, but at any rate we all did it. We then drank to the memory of the good Master Richard Watts. And I wish his Ghost may never have had worse usage under that roof than it had from us.

It was the witching time for Story-telling. "Our whole life, Travellers," said I, "is a story more or less intelligible, —generally less; but we shall read it by a clearer light when it is ended. I, for one, am so divided this night between fact and fiction, that I scarce know which is which. Shall I beguile the time by telling you a story as we sit here?"

They all answered, yes. I had little to tell them, but I was bound by my own proposal. Therefore, after looking for awhile at the spiral column of smoke wreathing up from my brown beauty, through which I could have almost sworn I saw the effigy of Master Richard Watts less startled than usual, I fired away.

CHAPTER II
The Story of Richard Doubledick

In the year one thousand seven hundred and ninety-nine, a relative of mine came limping down, on foot, to this town of Chatham. I call it this town, because if anybody present knows to a nicety where Rochester ends and Chatham begins, it is more than I do. He was a poor traveller, with not a farthing in his pocket. He sat by the fire in this very room, and he slept one night in a bed that will be occupied tonight by some one here.

My relative came down to Chatham to enlist in a cavalry regiment, if a cavalry regiment would have him; if not, to take King George's shilling from any corporal or sergeant who would put a bunch of ribbons in his hat. His object was to get shot; but he thought he might as well ride to death as be at the trouble of walking.

My relative's Christian name was Richard, but he was

better known as Dick. He dropped his own surname on the road down, and took up that of Doubledick. He was passed as Richard Doubledick; age, twenty-two; height, five foot ten; native place, Exmouth, which he had never been near in his life. There was no cavalry in Chatham when he limped over the bridge here with half a shoe to his dusty feet, so he enlisted into a regiment of the line, and was glad to get drunk and forget all about it.

You are to know that this relative of mine had gone wrong, and run wild. His heart was in the right place, but it was sealed up. He had been betrothed to a good and beautiful girl, whom he had loved better than she—or perhaps even he—believed; but in an evil hour he had given her cause to say to him solemnly, "Richard, I will never marry another man. I will live single for your sake, but Mary Marshall's lips"—her name was Mary Marshall —"never address another word to you on earth. Go, Richard! Heaven forgive you!" This finished him. This brought him down to Chatham. This made him Private Richard Doubledick, with a determination to be shot.

There was not a more dissipated and reckless soldier in Chatham barracks, in the year one thousand seven hundred and ninety-nine, than Private Richard Doubledick. He associated with the dregs of every regiment; he was as seldom sober as he could be, and was constantly under punishment. It became clear to the whole barracks that Private Richard Doubledick would very soon be flogged.

Now the Captain of Richard Doubledick's company was a young gentleman not above five years his senior, whose eyes had an expression in them which affected

Private Richard Doubledick in a very remarkable way. They were bright, handsome, dark eyes, —what are called laughing eyes generally, and, when serious, rather steady than severe,—but they were the only eyes now left in his narrowed world that Private Richard Doubledick could not stand. Unabashed by evil report and punishment, defiant of everything else and everybody else, he had but to know that those eyes looked at him for a moment, and he felt ashamed. He could not so much as salute Captain Taunton in the street like any other officer. He was reproached and confused, —troubled by the mere possibility of the captain's looking at him. In his worst moments, he would rather turn back, and go any distance out of his way, than encounter those two handsome, dark, bright eyes.

One day, when Private Richard Doubledick came out of the Black hole, where he had been passing the last eight-and-forty hours, and in which retreat he spent a good deal of his time, he was ordered to betake himself to Captain Taunton's quarters. In the stale and squalid state of a man just out of the Black hole, he had less fancy than ever for being seen by the Captain; but he was not so mad yet as to disobey orders, and consequently went up to the terrace overlooking the parade-ground, where the officers' quarters were; twisting and breaking in his hands, as he went along, a bit of the straw that had formed the decorative furniture of the Black hole.

"Come in!" cried the Captain, when he knocked with his knuckles at the door. Private Richard Doubledick pulled off his cap, took a stride forward, and felt very conscious that he stood in the light of the dark, bright eyes.

There was a silent pause. Private Richard Doubledick had put the straw in his mouth, and was gradually doubling it up into his windpipe and choking himself.

"Doubledick," said the Captain, "do you know where you are going to?"

"To the Devil, sir?" faltered Doubledick.

"Yes," returned the Captain. "And very fast."

Private Richard Doubledick turned the straw of the Black hole in his mouth, and made a miserable salute of acquiescence.

"Doubledick," said the Captain, "since I entered his Majesty's service, a boy of seventeen, I have been pained to see many men of promise going that road; but I have never been so pained to see a man determined to make the shameful journey as I have been, ever since you joined the regiment, to see you."

Private Richard Doubledick began to find a film stealing over the floor at which he looked; also to find the legs of the Captain's breakfast-table turning crooked, as if he saw them through water.

"I am only a common soldier, sir," said he. "It signifies very little what such a poor brute comes to."

"You are a man," returned the Captain, with grave indignation, "of education and superior advantages; and if you say that, meaning what you say, you have sunk lower than I had believed. How low that must be, I leave you to consider, knowing what I know of your disgrace, and seeing what I see."

"I hope to get shot soon, sir," said Private Richard Doubledick; "and then the regiment and the world together will be rid of me."

The legs of the table were becoming very crooked. Doubledick, looking up to steady his vision, met the eyes that had so strong an influence over him. He put his hand before his own eyes, and the breast of his disgrace-jacket swelled as if it would fly asunder.

"I would rather," said the young Captain, "see this in you, Doubledick, than I would see five thousand guineas counted out upon this table for a gift to my good mother. Have you a mother?"

"I am thankful to say she is dead, sir."

"If your praises," returned the Captain, "were sounded from mouth to mouth through the whole regiment, through the whole army, through the whole country, you would wish she had lived to say, with pride and joy, 'He is my son!'"

"Spare me, sir," said Doubledick. "She would never have heard any good of me. She would never have had any pride and joy in owning herself my mother. Love and compassion she might have had, and would have always had, I know; but not—Spare me, sir! I am a broken wretch, quite at your mercy!" And he turned his face to the wall, and stretched out his imploring hand.

"My friend—" began the Captain.

"God bless you, sir," sobbed Private Richard Doubledick.

"You are at the crisis of your fate. Hold your course unchanged a little longer, and you know what must happen. *I* know even better than you can imagine, that, after that has happened, you are lost. No man who could shed those tears could bear those marks."

"I fully believe it, sir," in a low, shivering voice said Private Richard Doubledick.

"But a man in any station can do his duty," said the young Captain, "and, in doing it, can earn his own respect, even if his case should be so very unfortunate and so very rare that he can earn no other man's. A common soldier, poor brute though you called him just now, has this advantage in the stormy times we live in, that he always does his duty before a host of sympathizing witnesses. Do you doubt that he may so do it as to be extolled through a whole regiment, through a whole army, through a whole country? Turn while you may yet retrieve the past, and try."

"I will! I ask for only one witness, sir," cried Richard, with a bursting heart.

"I understand you. I will be a watchful and a faithful one."

I have heard from Private Richard Doubledick's own lips, that he dropped down upon his knee, kissed that officer's hand, arose, and went out of the light of the dark, bright eyes, an altered man.

In that year, one thousand seven hundred and ninety-nine, the French were in Egypt, in Italy, in Germany, where not? Napoleon Bonaparte had likewise begun to stir against us in India, and most men could read the signs of the great troubles that were coming on. In the very next year, when we formed an alliance with Austria against him, Captain Taunton's regiment was on service in India. And there was not a finer non-commissioned officer in it, —no, nor in the whole line—than Corporal Richard Doubledick.

In eighteen hundred and one, the Indian army were on the coast of Egypt. Next year was the year of the proclamation of the short peace, and they were recalled. It had then become well known to thousands of men, that wherever Captain Taunton, with the dark, bright eyes, led, there, close to him, ever at his side, firm as a rock, true as the sun, and brave as Mars, would be certain to be found, while life beat in their hearts, that famous soldier, Sergeant Richard Doubledick.

Eighteen hundred and five, besides being the great year of Trafalgar, was a year of hard fighting in India. That year saw such wonders done by a Sergeant-Major, who cut his way single-handed through a solid mass of men, recovered the colours of his regiment, which had been seized from the hand of a poor boy shot through the heart, and rescued his wounded Captain, who was down, and in a very jungle of horses' hoofs and sabers,—saw such wonders done, I say, by this brave Sergeant-Major, that he was specially made the bearer of the colours he had won; and Ensign Richard Doubledick had risen from the ranks.

Sorely cut up in every battle, but always reinforced by the bravest of men, —for the fame of following the old colors, shot through and through, which Ensign Richard Doubledick had saved, inspired all breasts, —this regiment fought its way through the Peninsular war, up to the investment of Badajos in eighteen hundred and twelve.

Again and again it had been cheered through the British ranks until the tears had sprung into men's eyes at the mere hearing of the mighty British voice, so exultant in their valour; and there was not a drummer-boy but knew the legend, that wherever the two friends, Major Taunton, with the dark, bright eyes, and Ensign Richard Doubledick, who was devoted to him, were seen to go, there the boldest spirits in the English army became wild to follow.

One day, at Badajos, —not in the great storming, but in repelling a hot sally of the besieged upon our men at work in the trenches, who had given way, —the two officers found themselves hurrying forward, face to face, against a party of French infantry, who made a stand. There was an officer at their head, encouraging his men, —a courageous, handsome, gallant officer of five-and-thirty, whom Doubledick saw hurriedly, almost momentarily, but saw well. He particularly noticed this officer waving his sword, and rallying his men with an eager and excited cry, when they fired in obedience to his gesture, and Major Taunton dropped.

It was over in ten minutes more, and Doubledick returned to the spot where he had laid the best friend man ever had on a coat spread upon the wet clay. Major Taunton's uniform was opened at the breast, and on his shirt were three little spots of blood.

"Dear Doubledick," said he, "I am dying."

"For the love of Heaven, no!" exclaimed the other, kneeling down beside him, and passing his arm round his neck to raise his head. "Taunton! My preserver, my guardian angel, my witness! Dearest, truest, kindest of human beings! Taunton! For God's sake!"

The bright, dark eyes—so very, very dark now, in the pale face—smiled upon him; and the hand he had kissed thirteen years ago laid itself fondly on his breast.

"Write to my mother. You will see Home again. Tell her how we became friends. It will comfort her, as it comforts me."

He spoke no more, but faintly signed for a moment towards his hair as it fluttered in the wind. The Ensign understood him. He smiled again when he saw that, and, gently turning his face over on the supporting arm as if for rest, died, with his hand upon the breast in which he had revived a soul.

No dry eye looked on Ensign Richard Doubledick that melancholy day. He buried his friend on the field, and became a lone, bereaved man. Beyond his duty he appeared to have but two remaining cares in life, —one, to preserve the little packet of hair he was to give to Taunton's mother; the other, to encounter that French officer who had rallied the men under whose fire Taunton fell. A new legend now began to circulate among our troops; and it was, that when he and the French officer came face to face once more, there would be weeping in France.

The war went on—and through it went the exact picture of the French officer on the one side, and the bodily reality upon the other—until the Battle of Toulouse was fought. In the returns sent home appeared these words: "Severely wounded, but not dangerously, Lieutenant Richard Doubledick."

At Midsummer-time, in the year eighteen hundred and fourteen, Lieutenant Richard Doubledick, now a browned soldier, seven-and-thirty years of age, came home to England invalided. He brought the hair with him, near his heart. Many a French officer had he seen since that day; many a dreadful night, in searching with men and lanterns for his wounded, had he relieved French officers lying disabled; but the mental picture and the reality had never come together.

Though he was weak and suffered pain, he lost not an hour in getting down to Frome in Somersetshire, where Taunton's mother lived. In the sweet, compassionate words that naturally present themselves to the mind to-night, "he was the only son of his mother, and she was a widow."

It was a Sunday evening, and the lady sat at her quiet garden-window, reading the Bible; reading to herself, in a trembling voice, that very passage in it, as I have heard him tell. He heard the words: "Young man, I say unto thee, arise!"

He had to pass the window; and the bright, dark eyes of his debased time seemed to look at him. Her heart told her who he was; she came to the door quickly, and fell upon his neck.

"He saved me from ruin, made me a human creature, won me from infamy and shame. O, God for ever bless him! As He will, He will!"

"He will!" the lady answered. "I know he is in Heaven!" Then she piteously cried, "But O, my darling boy, my darling boy!"

Never from the hour when Private Richard Doubledick enlisted at Chatham had the Private, Corporal, Sergeant, Sergeant-Major, Ensign, or Lieutenant breathed his right name, or the name of Mary Marshall, or a word of the story of his life, into any ear except his reclaimer's. That previous scene in his existence was closed. He had firmly resolved that his expiation should be to live unknown; to disturb no more the peace that had long grown over his old offenses; to let it be revealed, when he was dead, that he had striven and suffered, and had never forgotten; and then, if they could forgive him and believe him—well, it would be time enough—time enough!

But that night, remembering the words he had cherished for two years, "Tell her how we became friends. It will comfort her, as it comforts me," he related everything. It gradually seemed to him as if in his maturity he had recovered a mother; it gradually seemed to her as if in her bereavement she had found a son. During his stay in England, the quiet garden into which he had slowly and painfully crept, a stranger, became the boundary of his home; when he was able to rejoin his regiment in the spring, he left the garden, thinking was this indeed the first time he had ever turned his face towards the old colors with a woman's blessing!

He followed them—so ragged, so scarred and pierced now, that they would scarcely hold together—to Quatre Bras and Ligny. He stood beside them, in an awful stillness of many men, shadowy through the mist and drizzle of a wet June forenoon, on the field of Waterloo. And down to that hour the picture in his mind of the French officer had never been compared with the reality.

The famous regiment was in action early in the battle, and received its first check in many an eventful year, when he was seen to fall. But it swept on to avenge him, and left behind it no such creature in the world of consciousness as Lieutenant Richard Doubledick.

Through pits of mire, and pools of rain; along deep ditches, once roads, that were pounded and ploughed to pieces by artillery, heavy wagons, tramp of men and horses, and the struggle of every wheeled thing that could carry wounded soldiers; jolted among the dying and the dead, so disfigured by blood and mud as to be hardly recognizable for humanity; undisturbed by the moaning of men and the shrieking of horses, which, newly taken from the peaceful pursuits of life, could not endure the sight of the stragglers lying by the wayside, never to resume their toilsome journey; dead, as to any sentient life that was in it, and yet, alive, —the form that had been Lieutenant Richard Doubledick, with whose praises England rang, was conveyed to Brussels. There it was tenderly laid down in hospital; and there it lay, week after week, through the long, bright summer days, until the harvest, spared by war, had ripened and was gathered in.

Over and over again the sun rose and set upon the crowded city; over and over again the moonlight nights were quiet on the plains of Waterloo: and all that time was a blank to what had been Lieutenant Richard Doubledick. Rejoicing troops marched into Brussels, and marched out; brothers and fathers, sisters, mothers, and wives, came thronging thither, drew their lots of joy or agony, and departed; so many times a day the bells rang; so many times the shadows of the great buildings changed; so many lights sprang up at dusk; so many feet passed here and there upon the pavements; so many hours of sleep and cooler air of night succeeded: indifferent to all, a marble face lay on a bed like the face of a recumbent statue on the tomb of Lieutenant Richard Doubledick.

Slowly laboring, at last, through a long, heavy dream of confused time and place, presenting faint glimpses of army surgeons whom he knew, and of faces that had been familiar to his youth, —dearest and kindest among them, Mary Marshall's, with a solicitude upon it more like reality than anything he could discern,—Lieutenant Richard Doubledick came back to life. To the beautiful life of a calm autumn evening sunset, to the peaceful life of a fresh, quiet room with a large window standing open; a balcony beyond, in which were moving leaves and sweet-smelling flowers; beyond, again, the clear sky, with the sun full in his sight, pouring its golden radiance on his bed.

It was so tranquil and so lovely that he thought he had passed into another world. And he said in a faint voice. "Taunton, are you near me?"

A face bent over him. Not his, his mother's.

"I came to nurse you. We have nursed you many weeks. You were moved here long ago. Do you remember nothing?"

"Nothing."

The lady kissed his cheek, and held his hand, soothing him.

"Where is the regiment? What has happened? Let me call you mother. What has happened, mother?"

"A great victory, dear. The war is over, and the regiment was the bravest in the field."

His eyes kindled, his lips trembled, he sobbed, and the tears ran down his face. He was very weak, too weak to move his hand.

"Was it dark just now?" he asked presently.

"No."

"It was only dark to me? Something passed away, like a black shadow. But as it went, and the sun—O the blessed sun, how beautiful it is! —touched my face, I thought I saw a light white cloud pass out at the door. Was there nothing that went out?"

She shook her head, and in a little while he fell asleep, she still holding his hand, and soothing him.

From that time, he recovered. Slowly, for he had been desperately wounded in the head, and had been shot in the body, but making some little advance every day. When he had gained sufficient strength to converse as he lay in bed, he soon began to remark that Mrs. Taunton always brought him back to his own history. Then he recalled his preserver's dying words, and thought, "It comforts her."

One day he awoke out of a sleep, refreshed, and asked her to read to him. But the curtain of the bed, softening the light, which she always drew back when he awoke, that she might see him from her table at the bedside where she sat at work, was held undrawn; and a woman's voice spoke, which was not hers.

"Can you bear to see a stranger?" it said softly. "Will you like to see a stranger?"

"Stranger!" he repeated. The voice awoke old memories, before the days of Private Richard Doubledick.

"A stranger now, but not a stranger once," it said in tones that thrilled him. "Richard, dear Richard, lost through so many years, my name—"

He cried out her name, "Mary," and she held him in her arms, and his head lay on her bosom.

"I am not breaking a rash vow, Richard. These are not Mary Marshall's lips that speak. I have another name."

She was married.

"I have another name, Richard. Did you ever hear it?"

"Never!"

He looked into her face, so pensively beautiful, and wondered at the smile upon it through her tears.

"Think again, Richard. Are you sure you never heard my altered name?"

"Never!"

"Don't move your head to look at me, dear Richard. Let it lie here, while I tell my story. I loved a generous, noble man; loved him with my whole heart; loved him for years and years; loved him faithfully, devotedly; loved him with no hope of return; loved him, knowing nothing of his highest qualities—not even knowing that he was alive. He was a brave soldier. He was honored and beloved by thousands of thousands, when the mother of his dear friend found me, and showed me that in all his triumphs he had never forgotten me. He was wounded in a great battle. He was brought, dying, here, into Brussels. I came to watch and tend him, as I would have joyfully gone, with such a purpose, to the dreariest ends of the earth. When he knew no one else, he knew me. When he suffered most, he bore his sufferings barely murmuring, content to rest his head where yours rests now. When he lay at the point of death, he married me, that he might call me Wife before he died. And the name, my dear love, that I took on that forgotten night—"

"I know it now!" he sobbed. "The shadowy remembrance strengthens. It is come back. I thank Heaven that my mind is quite restored! My Mary, kiss me; lull this weary head to rest, or I shall die of gratitude. His parting words were fulfilled. I see Home again!"

Well! They were happy. It was a long recovery, but they were happy through it all. The snow had melted on the ground, and the birds were singing in the leafless thickets of the early spring, when those three were first able to ride out together, and when people flocked about the open carriage to cheer and congratulate Captain Richard Doubledick.

But even then it became necessary for the Captain, instead of returning to England, to complete his recovery in the climate of Southern France. They found a spot upon the Rhone, within a ride of the old town of Avignon, and within view of its broken bridge, which was all they could desire; they lived there, together, six months; then returned to England. Mrs. Taunton, growing old after three years—though not so old as that her bright, dark eyes were dimmed—and remembering that her strength had been benefited by the change, resolved to go back for a year to those parts. So she went with a faithful servant, who had often carried her son in his arms; and she was to be rejoined and escorted home, at the year's end, by Captain Richard Doubledick.

She wrote regularly to her children (as she called them now), and they to her. She went to the neighborhood of Aix; and there, in their own chateau near the farmer's house she rented, she grew into intimacy with a family belonging to that part of France. The intimacy began in her often meeting among the vineyards a pretty child, a girl with a most compassionate heart, who was never tired of listening to the solitary English lady's stories of her poor son and the cruel wars. The family were as gentle as the child, and at length she came to know them so well that she accepted their invitation to pass the last month of her residence abroad under their roof. All this intelligence she wrote home, piecemeal as it came about, from time to time; and at last enclosed a polite note, from the head of the chateau, soliciting, on the occasion of his approaching mission to that neighborhood, the honor of the company of cet homme si justement célèbre, Monsieur le Capitaine Richard Doubledick.

Captain Doubledick, now a hardy, handsome man in the full vigor of life, broader across the chest and shoulders than he had ever been before, despatched a courteous reply, and followed it in person. Travelling through all that extent of country after three years of Peace, he blessed the better days on which the world had fallen. The corn was golden, not drenched in unnatural red; was bound in sheaves for food, not trodden underfoot by men in mortal fight. The smoke rose up from peaceful hearths, not blazing ruins. The carts were laden with the fair fruits of the earth, not with wounds and death. To him who had so often seen the terrible reverse, these things were beautiful indeed; and they brought him in a softened spirit of the old chateau near Aix upon a deep blue evening.

It was a large chateau of the genuine old ghostly kind, with round towers, and extinguishers, and a high leaden roof, and more windows than Aladdin's Palace. The lattice blinds were all thrown open after the heat of the day, and there were glimpses of rambling walls and corridors within. Then there were immense out-buildings fallen into partial decay, masses of dark trees, terrace-gardens, balustrades; tanks of water, too weak to play and too dirty to work; statues, weeds, and thickets of iron railing that seemed to have overgrown themselves like the shrubberies, and to have branched out in all manner of wild shapes. The entrance doors stood open, as doors often do in that country when the heat of the day is past; and the Captain saw no bell or knocker, and walked in.

He walked into a lofty stone hall, refreshingly cool and gloomy after the glare of a Southern day's travel. Extending along the four sides of this hall was a gallery, leading to suites of rooms; and it was lighted from the top. Still no bell was to be seen.

"Faith," said the Captain halting, ashamed of the clanking of his boots, "this is a ghostly beginning!"

He started back, and felt his face turn white. In the gallery, looking down at him, stood the French officer— the officer whose picture he had carried in his mind so long and so far. Compared with the original, at last—in every lineament how like it was!

He moved, and disappeared, and Captain Richard Doubledick heard his steps coming quickly down into the hall. He entered through an archway. There was a bright, sudden look upon his face, much such a look as it had worn in that fatal moment.

Monsieur le Capitaine Richard Doubledick? Enchanted to receive him! A thousand apologies! The servants were all out in the air. There was a little fete among them in the garden. In effect, it was the fete day of my daughter, the little cherished and protected of Madame Taunton.

He was so gracious and so frank that Monsieur le Capitaine Richard Doubledick could not withhold his hand. "It is the hand of a brave Englishman," said the French officer, retaining it while he spoke. "I could respect a brave Englishman, even as my foe, how much more as my friend! I also am a soldier!"

"He has not remembered me, as I have remembered him; he did not take such note of my face, that day, as I took of his," thought Captain Richard Doubledick. "How shall I tell him?"

The French officer conducted his guest into a garden and presented him to his wife, an engaging and beautiful woman, sitting with Mrs. Taunton in a whimsical old-fashioned pavilion. His daughter, her fair young face beaming with joy, came running to embrace him; and there was a boy-baby to tumble down among the orange trees on the broad steps, in making for his father's legs. A multitude of children visitors were dancing to sprightly music; and all the servants and peasants about the chateau were dancing too. It was a scene of innocent happiness that might have been invented for the climax of the scenes of peace which had soothed the Captain's journey.

He looked on, greatly troubled in his mind, until a resounding bell rang, and the French officer begged to show him his rooms. They went upstairs into the gallery from which the officer had looked down; and Monsieur le Capitaine Richard Doubledick was cordially welcomed to a grand outer chamber, and a smaller one within, all clocks and draperies, and hearths, and brazen dogs, and tiles, and cool devices, and elegance, and vastness.

"You were at Waterloo," said the French officer.

"I was," said Captain Richard Doubledick. "And at Badajos."

Left alone with the sound of his own stern voice in his ears, he sat down to consider, What shall I do, and how shall I tell him? At that time, unhappily, many deplorable duels had been fought between English and French officers, arising out of the recent war; and these duels, and how to avoid this officer's hospitality, were the uppermost thought in Captain Richard Doubledick's mind.

He was thinking, and letting the time run out in which he should have dressed for dinner, when Mrs. Taunton spoke to him outside the door, asking if he could give her the letter he had brought from Mary. "His mother, above all," the Captain thought. "How shall I tell *her?*"

"You will form a friendship with your host, I hope," said Mrs. Taunton, whom he hurriedly admitted, "that will last for life. He is so true-hearted and so generous,

Richard, that you can hardly fail to esteem one another. If He had been spared," she kissed (not without tears) the locket in which she wore his hair, "he would have appreciated him with his own magnanimity, and would have been truly happy that the evil days were past which made such a man his enemy."

She left the room; and the Captain walked, first to one window, whence he could see the dancing in the garden, then to another, whence he could see the smiling prospect and the peaceful vineyards.

"Spirit of my departed friend," said he, "is it through thee these better thoughts are rising in my mind? Is it thou who hast shown me, all the way I have been drawn to meet this man, the blessings of the altered time? Is it thou who hast sent thy stricken mother to me, to stay my angry hand? Is it from thee the whisper comes, that this man did his duty as thou didst, —and as I did, through thy guidance, which has wholly saved me here on earth, —and that he did no more?"

He sat down, with his head buried in his hands, and, when he rose up, made the second strong resolution of his life, —that neither to the French officer, nor to the mother of his departed friend, nor to any soul, while either of the two was living, would he breathe what only he knew. And when he touched that French officer's glass with his own, that day at dinner, he secretly forgave him in the name of the Divine Forgiver of injuries.

Here I ended my story as the first Poor Traveller. But, if I had told it now, I could have added that the time has since come when the son of Major Richard Doubledick, and the son of that French officer, friends as their fathers were before them, fought side by side in one cause, with their respective nations, like long-divided brothers whom the better times have brought together, fast united.

CHAPTER III
The Road

My story being finished, and the Wassail too, we broke up as the Cathedral bell struck Twelve. I did not take leave of my travellers that night; for it had come into my head to reappear, in conjunction with some hot coffee, at seven in the morning.

As I passed along the High Street, I heard the Waits at a distance, and struck off to find them. They were playing near one of the old gates of the City, at the corner of a wonderfully quaint row of red-brick tenements, which the clarionet obligingly informed me were inhabited by the Minor-Canons. They had odd little porches over the doors, like sounding-boards over old pulpits; and I thought I should like to see one of the Minor-Canons come out upon his top step, and favor us with a little Christmas discourse about the poor scholars of Rochester; taking for his text the words of his Master relative to the devouring of Widows' houses.

The clarionet was so communicative, and my inclinations were (as they generally are) of so vagabond a tendency, that I accompanied the Waits across an open green called the Vines, and assisted—in the French sense—at the performance of two waltzes, two polkas, and three

Irish melodies, before I thought of my inn any more. However, I returned to it then, and found a fiddle in the kitchen, and Ben, the wall-eyed young man, and two chambermaids, circling round the great deal table with the utmost animation.

I had a very bad night. It cannot have been owing to the turkey or the beef, —and the Wassail is out of the question, —but in every endeavor that I made to get to sleep I failed most dismally. I was never asleep; and in whatsoever unreasonable direction my mind rambled, the effigy of Master Richard Watts perpetually embarrassed it.

In a word, I only got out of the Worshipful Master Richard Watt's way by getting out of bed in the dark at six o'clock, and tumbling, as my custom is, into all the cold water that could be accumulated for the purpose. The outer air was dull and cold enough in the street, when I came down there; and the one candle in our supper-room at Watts's Charity looked as pale in the burning as if it had had a bad night too. But my Travellers had all slept soundly, and they took to the hot coffee, and the piles of bread-and-butter, which Ben had arranged like deals in a timber-yard, as kindly as I could desire.

While it was yet scarcely daylight, we all came out into the street together, and there shook hands. The widow took the little sailor towards Chatham, where he was to find a steamboat for Sheerness; the lawyer, with an extremely knowing look, went his own way, without committing himself by announcing his intentions; two more struck off by the cathedral and old castle for Maidstone;

and the book-peddler accompanied me over the bridge. As for me, I was going to walk by Cobham Woods, as far upon my way to London as I fancied.

When I came to the stile and footpath by which I was to diverge from the main road, I bade farewell to my last remaining Poor Traveller, and pursued my way alone. And now the mists began to rise in the most beautiful manner, and the sun to shine; and as I went on through the bracing air, seeing the hoar-frost sparkle everywhere, I felt as if all Nature shared in the joy of the great Birthday.

Going through the woods, the softness of my tread upon the mossy ground and among the brown leaves enhanced the Christmas sacredness by which I felt surrounded. As the whitened stems environed me, I thought how the Founder of the time had never raised his benignant hand, save to bless and heal, except in the case of one unconscious tree. By Cobham Hall, I came to the village, and the churchyard where the dead had been quietly buried, "in the sure and certain hope" which Christmastime inspired. What children could I see at play, and not be loving of, recalling who had loved them! No garden that I passed was out of unison with the day, for I remembered that the tomb was in a garden, and that "she, supposing him to be the gardener," had said, "Sir, if thou have borne him hence, tell me where thou hast laid him, and I will take him away." In time, the distant river with the ships came full in view, and with it pictures of the poor fishermen, mending their nets, who arose and followed him, —of the teaching of the people from a ship pushed off a little way from shore, by reason of the multitude,

—of a majestic figure walking on the water, in the loneliness of night. My very shadow on the ground was eloquent of Christmas; for did not the people lay their sick where the mere shadows of the men who had heard and seen him might fall as they passed along?

Thus Christmas begirt me, far and near, until I had come to Blackheath, and had walked down the long vista of gnarled old trees in Greenwich Park, and was being steam-rattled through the mists now closing in once more, towards the lights of London. Brightly they shone, but not so brightly as my own fire, and the brighter faces around it, when we came together to celebrate the day. And there I told of worthy Master Richard Watts, and of my supper with the Six Poor Travellers who were neither Rogues nor Proctors, and from that hour to this I have never seen one of them again.

THE HOLLY-TREE

Three Branches
FIRST BRANCH
Myself

 have kept one secret in the course of my life. I am a bashful man. Nobody would suppose it, nobody ever does suppose it, nobody ever did suppose it, but I am naturally a bashful man. This is the secret which I have never breathed until now.

I might greatly move the reader by some account of the innumerable places I have not been to, the innumerable people I have not called upon or received, the innumerable social evasions I have been guilty of, solely because I am by original constitution and character a bashful man. But I will leave the reader unmoved, and proceed with the object before me.

That object is to give a plain account of my travels and discoveries in the Holly-Tree Inn; in which place of good entertainment for man and beast I was once snowed up.

It happened in the memorable year when I parted for ever from Angela Leath, whom I was shortly to have married, on making the discovery that she preferred my bosom friend. From our schooldays I had freely admitted Edwin, in my own mind, to be far superior to myself; and, though I was grievously wounded at heart, I felt the preference to be natural, and tried to forgive them both. It was under these circumstances that I resolved to go to America—on my way to the Devil.

Communicating my discovery neither to Angela nor to Edwin, but resolving to write each of them an affecting letter conveying my blessing and forgiveness, which the steam-tender for shore should carry to the post when I myself should be bound for the New World, far beyond recall, —I say, locking up my grief in my own breast, and consoling myself as I could with the prospect of being generous, I quietly left all I held dear, and started on the desolate journey I have mentioned.

The dead winter-time was in full dreariness when I left my chambers for ever, at five o'clock in the morning. I had shaved by candlelight, of course, and was miserably cold, and experienced that general all-pervading sensation of getting up to be hanged which I have usually found inseparable from untimely rising under such circumstances.

How well I remember the forlorn aspect of Fleet Street when I came out of the Temple! The street-lamps flickered in the gusty northeast wind, as if the very gas were contorted with cold; the white-topped houses; bleak, star-lighted sky; the market people and other early stragglers, trotting to circulate their almost frozen blood; the hospitable light and warmth of the few coffeeshops and public-houses that were open for such customers; the hard, dry, frosty rime with which the air was charged (the wind had already beaten it into every crevice), and which lashed my face like a steel whip.

It wanted nine days to the end of the month, and end of the year. The Post-office packet for the United States was to depart from Liverpool, weather permitting, on the first of the ensuing month, and I had the intervening time on my hands. I had taken this into consideration, and had resolved to make a visit to a certain spot (which I need not name) on the farther borders of Yorkshire. It was endeared to me by my having first seen Angela at a farm-house in that place, and my melancholy was gratified by the idea of taking a wintry leave of it before my expatriation. I ought to explain, that, to avoid being sought out before my resolution should have been rendered irrevocable by being carried into full effect, I had written to Angela overnight, in my usual manner lamenting that urgent business, of which she should know all particulars by and by—took me unexpectedly away from her for a week or ten days.

There was no Northern Railway at that time, and in its place there were stage-coaches; which I occasionally find myself, in common with some other people, affecting to lament now, but which everybody dreaded as a very serious penance then. I had secured the box-seat on the fastest of these, and my business in Fleet Street was to get into a cab with my portmanteau, so to make the best of my way to the Peacock at Islington, where I was to join this coach. But when one of our Temple watchmen, who carried my portmanteau into Fleet Street for me, told me about the

huge blocks of ice that had for some days past been float-
ing in the river, having closed up in the night, and made a
walk from the Temple Gardens over to the Surrey shore, I
began to ask myself the question, whether the box-seat
would not be likely to put a sudden and a frosty end to my
unhappiness. I was heartbroken, it is true, and yet I was
not quite so far gone as to wish to be frozen to death.

When I got up to the Peacock, —where I found everybody drinking hot purl, in self-preservation, —I asked if
there were an inside seat to spare. I then discovered that,
inside or out, I was the only passenger. This gave me a
still livelier idea of the great inclemency of the weather,
since that coach always loaded particularly well. However, I took a little purl (which I found uncommonly
good), and got into the coach. When I was seated, they
built me up with straw to the waist, and, conscious of
making a rather ridiculous appearance, I began my journey.

It was still dark when we left the Peacock. For a little
while, pale, uncertain ghosts of houses and trees appeared
and vanished, and then it was hard, black, frozen day.
People were lighting their fires; smoke was mounting
straight up high into the rarefied air; and we were rattling
for Highgate Archway over the hardest ground I have
ever heard the ring of iron shoes on. As we got into the
country, everything seemed to have grown old and grey.
The roads, the trees, thatched roofs of cottages and home-
steads, the ricks in farmers' yards. Out-door work was
abandoned, horse-troughs at roadside inns were frozen
hard, no stragglers lounged about, doors were close shut,

little turnpike houses had blazing fires inside, and children (even turnpike people have children, and seem to like them) rubbed the frost from the little panes of glass with their chubby arms, that their bright eyes might catch a glimpse of the solitary coach going by. I don't know when the snow began to set in; but I know that we were changing horses somewhere when I heard the guard remark, "The old lady up in the sky was picking her geese pretty hard today." Then, indeed, I found the white down falling fast and thick.

The lonely day wore on, and I dozed it out, as a lonely traveller does. I was warm and valiant after eating and drinking,—particularly after dinner; cold and depressed at all other times. I was always bewildered as to time and place, and always more or less out of my senses. The coach and horses seemed to execute in chorus Auld Lang Syne, without a moment's intermission. They kept the time and tune with the greatest regularity, and rose into the swell at the beginning of the Refrain, with a precision that worried me to death. While we changed horses, the guard and coachman went stumping up and down the road, printing off their shoes in the snow, and poured so much liquid consolation into themselves without being any the worse for it, that I began to confound them, as it darkened again, with two great white casks standing on end. Our horses tumbled down in solitary places, and we got them up,—which was the pleasantest variety *I* had, for it warmed me. And it snowed and snowed, and still it snowed, and never left off snowing. All night long we went on in this manner. Thus we came round the clock,

upon the Great North Road, to the performance of Auld
Lang Syne all day again. And it snowed and snowed, and
still it snowed, and never left off snowing.

I forget now where we were at noon on the second day,
and where we ought to have been; but I know that we
were scores of miles behindhand; and that our case was
growing worse every hour. The drift was becoming
prodigiously deep; landmarks were getting snowed out;
the road and the fields were all one; instead of having
fences and hedgerows to guide us, we went crunching
on over an unbroken surface of ghastly white that might
sink beneath us at any moment and drop us down a
whole hillside. Still the coachman and guard—who kept
together on the box, always in council, and looking
well about them—made out the track with astonishing
sagacity.

When we came in sight of a town, it looked, to my
fancy, like a large drawing on a slate, with abundance of
slate-pencil expended on the churches and houses where
the snow lay thickest. When we came within a town, and
found the church clocks all stopped, the dial-faces choked
with snow, and the inn-signs blotted out, it seemed as if
the whole place were overgrown with white moss. As to
the coach, it was a mere snowball; similarly, the men and
boys who ran along beside us to the town's end, turning
our clogged wheels and encouraging our horses, were men
and boys of snow; and the bleak, wild solitude to which
they at last dismissed us was a snowy Sahara. One would
have thought this enough: notwithstanding which, I

pledge my word that it snowed, and snowed, and still it snowed, and never left off snowing.

We performed Auld Lang Syne the whole day; seeing nothing out of towns and villages, but the track of stoats, hares, and foxes, and sometimes of birds. At nine o'clock at night, on a Yorkshire moor, a cheerful burst from our horn, and a welcome sound of talking, with a glimmering and moving about of lanterns, roused me from my drowsy state. I found that we were going to change.

They helped me out, and I said to a waiter, whose bare head became as white as King Lear's in a single minute, "What Inn is this?"

"The Holly-Tree, sir," said he.

"Upon my word, I believe," said I, apologetically, to the guard and coachman, "that I must stop here."

Now the landlord, and the landlady, and the ostler, and the postboy, and all the stable authorities, had already asked the coachman, to the wide-eyed interest of all the rest of the establishment, if he meant to go on. The coachman had already replied, "Yes, he'd take her through it," —meaning by Her the coach,—"if so be as George would stand by him." George was the guard, and he had already sworn that he *would* stand by him. So the helpers were already getting the horses out.

My declaring myself beaten, after this parley, was not an announcement without preparation. Indeed, but for the way to the announcement being smoothed by the parley, I more than doubt whether, as an innately bashful man, I should have had the confidence to make it. As it was, it received the approval even of the guard and coachman.

Therefore, with many confirmations of my inclining, and many remarks from one bystander to another, that the gentleman could go for'ard by the mail tomorrow, whereas tonight he would only be froze, and where was the good of a gentleman being froze,—ah, let alone buried alive (which latter clause was added by a humorous helper as a joke at my expense, and was extremely well received), I saw my portmanteau got out stiff, like a frozen body; did the handsome thing by the guard and coachman; wished them goodnight and a prosperous journey; and, a little ashamed of myself, after all, for leaving them to fight it out alone, followed the landlord, landlady, and waiter of the Holly-Tree upstairs.

I thought I had never seen such a large room as that into which they showed me. It had five windows, with dark red curtains that would have absorbed the light of a general illumination; and there were complications of drapery at the top of the curtains, that went wandering about the wall in a most extraordinary manner. I asked for a smaller room, and they told me there was no smaller room. They could screen me in, however the landlord said. They brought a great old japanned screen, with natives (Japanese, I suppose) engaged in a variety of idotic pursuits all over it; and left me roasting whole before an immense fire.

My bedroom was some quarter of a mile off, up a great staircase at the end of a long gallery; and nobody knows what a misery this is to a bashful man who would rather not meet people on the stairs. It was the grimmest room I have ever had the nightmare in; and all the furniture, from the four posts of the bed to the two old silver candle-sticks, was tall, high-shouldered, and spindle-waisted. Below, in my sittingroom, if I looked round my screen, the wind rushed at me like a mad bull; if I stuck to my arm-chair, the fire scorched me to the color of a new brick. The chimney-piece was very high, and there was a bad glass—what I may call a wavy glass—above it, which, when I stood up, just showed me my anterior phrenological developments,—and these never look well, in any subject, cut short off at the eyebrow. If I stood with my back to the fire, a gloomy vault of darkness above and beyond the screen insisted on being looked at; and, in its dim remoteness, the drapery of the ten curtains of the five windows went twisting and creeping about, like a nest of gigantic worms.

I suppose that what I observe in myself must be observed by some other men of similar character in *themselves;* therefore I am emboldened to mention, that, when I travel, I never arrive at a place but I immediately want to go away from it. Before I had finished my supper of broiled fowl and mulled port, I had impressed upon the waiter in detail my arrangements for departure in the morning. Breakfast and bill at eight. Fly at nine. Two horses, or, if needful, even four.

Tired though I was, the night appeared about a week long. In oases of nightmare I thought of Angela, and felt more depressed than ever by the reflection that I was on the shortest road to Gretna Green. What had *I* to do with Gretna Green. I was not going *that* way to the Devil, but by the American route, I remarked in my bitterness.

In the morning I found that it was snowing still, that it had snowed all night, and that I was snowed up. Nothing could get out of that spot on the moor, or could come at it, until the road had been cut out by laborers from the market-town. When they might cut their way to the Holly-Tree nobody could tell me.

It was now Christmas-eve. I should have had a dismal Christmas-time of it anywhere, and consequently that did not so much matter; still, being snowed up was like dying of frost, a thing I had not bargained for. I felt very lonely. Yet I could no more have proposed to the landlord and landlady to admit me to their society (though I should have liked it very much) than I could have asked them to present me with a piece of plate. Here my great secret, the real bashfulness of my character, is to be observed. Like most bashful men, I judge of other people as if they were bashful too. Besides being far too shamefaced to make the proposal myself, I really had a delicate misgiving that it would be in the last degree disconcerting to them.

Trying to settle down, therefore, in my solitude, I first of all asked what books there were in the house. The waiter brought me a *Book of Roads,* two or three old Newspapers, a little Song-Book, terminating in a collection of Toasts and Sentiments, a little Jest-Book, an odd volume of *Peregrine Pickle,* and the *Sentimental Journey.* I knew every word of the two last already, but I read them through again, then tried to hum all the songs (Auld Lang Syne was among them); went entirely through the jokes,—in which I found a fund of melancholy adapted to my state of mind; proposed all the toasts, enunciated all the sentiments, and mastered the papers. The latter had nothing in them but stock advertisements, a meeting about a country rate and a highway robbery. As I am a greedy reader, I could not make this supply hold out until night; it was exhausted by teatime. Being then entirely cast upon my own resources, I got through an hour in considering what to do next. Ultimately, it came into my head (from which I was anxious by any means to exclude Angela and Edwin), that I would endeavor to recall my experience of Inns, and would try how long it lasted me. I stirred the fire, moved my chair a little to one side of the screen,—not daring to go far, for I knew the wind was waiting to make a rush at me, I could hear it growling,—and began.

My first impressions of an Inn dated from the Nursery; consequently I went back to the Nursery for a starting-point, and found myself at the knee of a sallow woman with a fishy eye, an aquiline nose, and a green gown, whose specialty was a dismal narrative of a landlord by the roadside, whose visitors unaccountably disappeared for many years, until it was discovered that the pursuit of his life had been to convert them into pies. For the better devotion of himself to this branch of industry, he had constructed a secret door behind the head of the bed; and when the visitor (oppressed with pie) had fallen asleep, this wicked landlord would look softly in with a lamp in one hand and a knife in the other, would cut his throat, and would make him into pies; for which purpose he had coppers, underneath a trap-door, always boiling; and rolled out his pastry in the dead of the night. Yet even he was not insensible to the stings of conscience, for he never went to sleep without being heard to mutter, "Too much pepper!" which was eventually the cause of his being brought to justice. I had no sooner disposed of this criminal than there started up another of the same period, whose profession was originally housebreaking; in the pursuit of which art he had had his right ear chopped off one night, as he was burglariously getting in at a window, by a brave and lovely servant-maid (whom the aquiline-nosed woman, though not at all answering the description, always mysteriously implied to be herself). After several years, this brave and lovely servant-maid was married to the landlord of a country Inn; which landlord had this remarkable characteristic, that he always wore a silk nightcap, and never would on any consideration take it off. At last, one night, when he was fast aseep, the brave and lovely woman lifted up his silk nightcap on the right side, and found that he had no ear there; upon which she sagaciously perceived that he was the clipped housebreaker, who had married her with the intention of putting her to death. She immediately heated the poker and terminated his career, for which she was taken to King George upon his throne, and received the compliments of royalty on her great discretion and valor. This same narrator, who had a Ghoulish pleasure, I have long been persuaded, in terrifying me to the utmost confines of my reason, had another authentic anecdote within her own experience, founded, I now believe, upon *Raymond and Agnes, or the Bleeding Nun.* She said it happened to her brother-in-law, who was immensely rich,—which my father was not; and immensely tall,—which my father was not. It

was always a point with this Ghoul to present my dearest
relations and friends to my youthful mind under circumstances of disparaging contrast. The brother-in-law was
riding once through a forest on a magnificent horse (we
had no magnificent horse at our house), attended by a
favorite and valuable Newfoundland dog (we had no
dog), when he found himself benighted, and came to an
Inn. A dark woman opened the door, and he asked her if
he could have a bed there. She answered yes, and put his
horse in the stable, and took him into a room where there
were two dark men. While he was at supper, a parrot in
the room began to talk, saying, "Blood, blood! Wipe up
the blood!" Upon which one of the dark men wrung the
parrot's neck, and said he was fond of roasted parrots, and
he meant to have this one for breakfast in the morning.
After eating and drinking heartily, the immensely rich,
tall brother-in-law went up to bed; but he was rather
vexed, because they had shut his dog in the stable, saying
that they never allowed dogs in the house. He sat very
quiet for more than an hour, thinking and thinking, when,
just as his candle was burning out, he heard a scratch at
the door. He opened the door, and there was the Newfoundland dog! The dog came softly in, smelt about him,
went straight to some straw in the corner which the dark
men had said covered apples, tore the straw away, and
disclosed two sheets steeped in blood. Just at that moment
the candle went out, and the brother-in-law, looking
through a chink in the door, saw the two dark men stealing upstairs; one armed with a dagger that long (about
five feet); the other carrying a chopper, a sack, and a

spade. Having no remembrance of the close of this adventure, I suppose my faculties to have been always so frozen with terror at this stage of it, that the power of listening stagnated within me for some quarter of an hour.

These barbarous stories carried me, sitting there on the Holly-Tree hearth, to the Roadside Inn, renowned in my time in a six-penny book with a folding plate, representing in a central compartment of oval form the portrait of Jonathan Bradford, and in four corner compartments four incidents of the tragedy with which the name is associated,—colored with a hand at once so free and economical, that the bloom of Jonathan's complexion passed without any pause into the breeches of the ostler, and, smearing itself off into the next division, became rum in a bottle. Then I remembered how the landlord was found at the murdered traveller's bedside, with his own knife at his feet, and blood upon his hand; how he was hanged for the murder, notwithstanding his protestation that he had indeed come there to kill the traveller for his saddle-bags, but had been stricken motionless on finding him already slain; and how the ostler, years afterwards, owned the deed. By this time I had made myself quite uncomfortable. I stirred the fire, and stood with my back to it as long as I could bear the heat, looking up at the darkness beyond the screen, and at the wormy curtains creeping in and creeping out, like the worms in the ballad of Alonzo the Brave and the Fair Imogene.

There was an Inn in the cathedral town where I went to school, which had pleasanter recollections about it than any of these. I took it next. It was the Inn where friends used to put up, and where we used to go to see parents, and to have salmon and fowls, and be tipped. It had an ecclesiastical sign,—the Mitre,—and a bar that seemed to be the next best thing to a bishopric, it was so snug. I loved the landlord's youngest daughter to distraction,— but let that pass. It was in this Inn that I was cried over by my rosy little sister, because I had acquired a black eye in a fight. And though she had been, that Holly-Tree night, for many a long year where all tears are dried, the Mitre softened me yet.

"To be continued tomorrow," said I, when I took my candle to go to bed. But my bed took it upon itself to continue the train of thought that night. It carried me away, like the enchanted carpet, to a distant place (though still in England), and there, alighting from a stage-coach at another Inn in the snow, as I had actually done some years before, I repeated in my sleep a curious experience I had really had here. More than a year before I made the journey in the course of which I put up at that Inn, I had lost a very near and dear friend by death. Every night since, at home or away from home, I had dreamed of that friend; sometimes as still living; sometimes as returning from the world of shadows to comfort me; always as being beautiful, placid, and happy, never in association with any approach to fear or distress. It was a lonely Inn in a wide moorland place, that I halted to pass the night. When I had looked from my bedroom window over the waste of snow on which the moon was shining, I sat down by my fire to write a letter. I had always, until that hour, kept it within my own breast that I dreamed every night of the dear lost one. But in the letter that I wrote I recorded the circumstance, and added that I felt much interested in proving whether the subject of my dream would still be faithful to me, travel-tired, and in that remote place. No. I lost the beloved figure of my vision in parting with the secret. My sleep has never looked upon it since, in sixteen years, but once. I was in Italy, and awoke (or seemed to awake), the well-remembered voice distinctly in my ears, conversing with it. I entreated it, as it rose above my bed and soared up to the vaulted roof of the old room, to answer me a question I had asked touching the Future Life. My hands were still outstretched towards it as it vanished, when I heard a bell ringing by the garden wall, and a voice in the deep stillness of the night calling on all good Christians to pray for the souls of the dead; it being All Souls' Eve.

To return to the Holly-Tree. When I awoke next day, it was freezing hard, and the lowering sky threatened more snow. My breakfast cleared away, I drew my chair into its former place, and, with the fire getting so much the better of the landscape that I sat in twilight, resumed my Inn remembrances.

That was a good Inn down in Wiltshire where I put up once, in the days of the hard Wiltshire ale, and before all beer was bitterness. It was on the skirts of Salisbury Plain, and the midnight wind that rattled my lattice window came moaning at me from Stonehenge. There was a hanger-on at that establishment (a supernaturally preserved Druid I believe him to have been, and to be still), with long white hair, and a flinty blue eye always looking afar off; who claimed to have been a shepherd, and who seemed to be ever watching for the reappearance, on the verge of the horizon, of some ghostly flock of sheep that had been mutton for many ages. He was a man with a weird belief in him that no one could count the stones of Stonehenge twice, and make the same number of them; likewise, that any one who counted them three times nine times, and then stood in the center and said, "I dare!" would behold a tremendous apparition, and be stricken dead. He pretended to have seen a bustard (I suspect him to have been familiar with the dodo), in manner following: He was out upon the plain at the close of a late autumn day, when he dimly discerned, going on before him at a curious, fitfully bounding pace, what he at first supposed to be a gig-umbrella that had been blown from some conveyance, but what he presently believed to be a lean dwarf upon a little pony. Having followed this object for some distance without gaining on it, and having called to it many times without receiving any answer, he pursued it for miles and miles, when, at length coming up with it, he discovered it to be the last bustard in Great Britain, degenerated into a wingless state, and running along the ground. Resolved to capture him or perish in the attempt, he closed with the bustard; but the bustard, who had formed a counter-resolution that he should do neither, threw him, stunned him, and was last seen making off due west. This weird man, at that stage of metempsychosis, may have been a sleep-walker or an enthusiast or a robber; but I awoke one night to find him in the dark at my bedside, repeating the Athanasian Creed in a terrific voice.

I paid my bill next day, and retired from the county with all possible precipitation.

That was not a commonplace story which worked itself out at a little Inn in Switzerland, while I was staying there. It was a very homely place, in a village of one narrow, zigzag street, among mountains, and you went in at the main door through the cowhouse, and among the mules and the dogs and the fowls, before ascending a great bare staircase to the rooms; which were all of unpainted wood, without plastering or papering,—like rough packing-cases. Outside there was nothing but the straggling street, a little toy church with a copper-colored steeple, a pine forest, a torrent, mists, and mountain-sides. A young man belonging to this Inn had disappeared eight weeks before (it was winter-time) and was supposed to have had some undiscovered love affair, and to have gone for a soldier. He had got up in the night, and dropped into the village street from the loft in which he slept with another man; and he had done it so quietly, that his companion and fellow-labourer had heard no movement when he was awakened in the morning, and they said, "Louis, where is Henri?" They looked for him high and low, in vain, and gave him up. Now, outside this Inn, there stood, as there stood outside every dwelling in the village, a stack of firewood; but the stack belonging to the Inn was higher than any of the rest, because the Inn was the richest house, and burnt the most fuel. It began to be noticed, while they were looking high and low, that a Bantam cock, part of the live stock of the Inn, put himself wonderfully out of his way to get to the top of this wood-stack; and that he would stay there for hours and hours, crowing, until he appeared in danger of splitting himself. Five weeks went on,—six weeks,—and still this terrible Bantam, neglecting his domestic affairs, was always on the top of the wood-stack, crowing the very eyes out of his head. By this time it was perceived that Louis had become inspired with a violent animosity towards the terrible Bantam, and one morning he was seen by a woman, who sat nursing her goitre at a little window in a gleam of sun, to catch up a rough billet of wood, with a great oath, hurl it at the terrible Bantam crowing on the wood-stack, and bring him down dead. Hereupon the woman, with a sudden light in her mind stole round to the back of the wood-stack, and, being a good climber, as all those women are, climbed up, and soon was seen upon the summit, scream-ing, looking down the hollow within, and crying, "Seize Louis, the murderer! Ring the church bell! Here is the body!" I saw the murderer that day, and I saw him as I sat by my fire at the Holly-Tree Inn, and I see him now, lying shackled with cords on the stable litter, among the mild eyes and the smoking breath of the cows, waiting to be taken away by the police, and stared at by the fearful village. A heavy animal,—the dullest animal in the sta-bles,—with a stupid head, and a lumpish face devoid of any trace of sensibility, who had been, within the knowl-edge of the murdered youth, an embezzler of certain small moneys belonging to his master, and who had taken this hopeful mode of putting a possible accuser out of his way. All of which he confessed next day, like a sulky wretch who couldn't be troubled any more, now that they had got

hold of him, and meant to make an end of him. I saw him
once again, on the day of my departure from the Inn. In
that Canton the headsman still does his office with a
sword; and I came upon this murderer sitting bound to a
chair, with his eyes bandaged, on a scaffold in a little
market-place. In that instant, a great sword (loaded with
quicksilver in the thick part of the blade) swept round
him like a gust of wind or fire, and there was no such
creature in the world. My wonder was, not that he was so
suddenly despatched, but that any head was left unreaped,
within a radius of fifty yards of that tremendous sickle.

That was a good Inn, too, with the kind, cheerful landlady and the honest landlord, where I lived in the shadow
of Mont Blanc, and where one of the apartments has a
zoological papering on the walls, not so accurately joined
but that the elephant occasionally rejoices in a tiger's hind
legs and tail, while the lion puts on a trunk and tusks, and
the bear, molting as it were, appears as to portions of
himself like a leopard. I made several American friends at
that Inn, who all called Mont Blanc Mount Blank,—except one good-humored gentleman, of a very sociable nature, who became on such intimate terms with it that he
spoke of it familiarly as "Blank;" observing, at breakfast,
"Blank looks pretty tall this morning;" or considerably
doubting in the courtyard in the evening, whether there
warn't some go-ahead naters in our country, sir, that
would make out the top of Blank in a couple of hours
from first start—now!

Once I passed a fortnight at an Inn in the North of
England, where I was haunted by the ghost of a tremen-

dous pie. It was a Yorkshire pie, like a fort,—an abandoned fort with nothing in it; but the waiter had a fixed idea that it was a point of ceremony at every meal to put the pie on the table. After some days I tried to hint, in several delicate ways, that I considered the pie done with; as, for example, by emptying fag-ends of glasses of wine into it; putting cheese-plates and spoons into it, as into a basket; putting wine-bottles into it, as into a cooler; but always in vain, the pie being invariably cleaned out again and brought up as before. At last, beginning to be doubtful whether I was not the victim of a spectral illusion, and whether my health and spirits might not sink under the horrors of an imaginary pie, I cut a triangle out of it, fully as large as the musical instrument of that name in a powerful orchestra. Human prevision could not have foreseen the result—but the waiter mended the pie. With some effectual species of cement, he adroitly fitted the triangle in again, and I paid my reckoning and fled.

The Holly-Tree was getting rather dismal. I made an overland expedition beyond the screen, and penetrated as far as the fourth window. Here I was driven back by stress of weather. Arrived at my winter-quarters once more, I made up the fire, and took another Inn.

It was in the remotest part of Cornwall. A great annual Miners' Feast was being holden at the Inn, when I and my travelling companions presented ourselves at night among the wild crowd that were dancing before it by torchlight. We had had a breakdown in the dark, on a stony morass some miles away; and I had the honor of leading one of the unharnessed post-horses. If any lady or gentleman, on perusal of the present lines, will take any very tall post-horse with his traces hanging about his legs, and will conduct him by the bearing-rein into the heart of a country dance of a hundred and fifty couples, that lady or gentleman will then, and only then, form an adequate idea of the extent to which that post-horse will tread on his conductor's toes. Over and above which, the post-horse, finding three hundred people whirling about him, will probably rear, and also lash out with his hind legs, in a manner incompatible with dignity or self-respect on his conductor's part. With such little drawbacks on my usually impressive aspect, I appeared at this Cornish Inn, to the unutterable wonder of the Cornish Miners. It was full, and twenty times full, and nobody could be received but the post-horse,—though to get rid of that noble animal was something. While my fellow-travellers and I were discussing how to pass the night and so much of the next day as must intervene before the jovial blacksmith and the jovial wheelwright would be in a condition to go out on the morass and mend the coach, an honest man stepped forth from the crowd and proposed his unlet floor of two rooms, with supper of eggs and bacon, ale and punch. We joyfully accompanied him home to the strangest of clean houses, where we were well entertained to the satisfaction of all parties. But the novel feature of the entertainment was, that our host was a chair-maker, and that the chairs assigned to us were mere frames, altogether without bottoms of any sort; so that we passed the evening on perches. Nor was this the absurdest consequence; for when we unbent at supper, and any one of us gave way to laughter, he forgot the peculiarity of his position, and instantly disappeared. I myself, doubled up into an attitude from which self-extrication was impossible, was taken out of my frame, like a clown in a comic pantomime who has tumbled into a tub, five times by the taper's light during the eggs and bacon.

The Holly-Tree was fast reviving within me a sense of loneliness. I began to feel conscious that my subject would never carry on until I was dug out. I might be a week here,—weeks!

There was a story with a singular idea in it, connected with an Inn I once passed a night at in a picturesque old town on the Welsh border. In a large double-bedded room of this Inn there had been a suicide committed by poison, in one bed, while a tired traveller slept unconscious in the other. After that time, the suicide bed was never used, but the other constantly was; the disused bedstead remaining in the room empty, though as to all other respects in its old state. The story ran, that whosoever slept in this room, though never so entire a stranger, from never so far off, was invariably observed to come down in the morning with an impression that he smelt Laudanum, and that his mind always turned upon the subject of suicide; to which, whatever kind of man he might be, he was certain to make some reference if he conversed with any one. This went on for years, until it at length induced the landlord to take the disused bedstead down, and bodily burn it,—bed, hangings, and all. The strange influence (this was the story) now changed to a fainter one, but never changed afterwards. The occupant of that room, with occasional

but very rare exceptions, would come down in the morning, trying to recall a forgotten dream he had had in the
night. The landlord, on his mentioning his perplexity,
would suggest various common-place subjects, not one of
which, as he very well knew, was the true subject. But the
moment the landlord suggested "Poison," the traveler
started, and cried, "Yes!" He never failed to accept that
suggestion, and he never recalled any more of the dream.

This reminiscence brought the Welsh Inns in general
before me; with the women in their round hats, and the
harpers with their white beards (venerable, but humbugs,
I am afraid), playing outside the door while I took my
dinner. The transition was natural to the Highland Inns,
with the oatmeal bannocks, the honey, the venison steaks,
the trout from the loch, the whisky, and perhaps (having
the materials so temptingly at hand) the Athol brose.
Once was I coming south from the Scottish Highlands in
hot haste, hoping to change quickly at the station at the
bottom of a certain wild historical glen, when these eyes
did with mortification see the landlord come out with a
telescope and sweep the whole prospect for the horses;
which horses were away picking up their own living, and
did not heave in sight under four hours. Having thought
of the loch-trout, I was taken by quick association to the
Anglers' Inns of England (I have assisted at innumerable
feats of angling by lying in the bottom of the boat, whole
summer days, doing nothing with the greatest perseverance; which I have generally found to be as effectual towards the taking of fish as the finest tackle and the utmost
science), and to the pleasant white, clean, flower-pot-deco-

rated bedrooms of those inns, overlooking the river, and
the ferry, and the green ait, and the church-spire, and the
country bridge; and to the peerless Emma with the bright
eyes and the pretty smile, who waited, bless her! with a
natural grace that would have converted Blue-Beard.
Casting my eyes upon my Holly-Tree fire, I next discerned
among the glowing coals the pictures of a score or more of
those wonderful English posting-inns which we are all so
sorry to have lost, which were so large and so comfortable, and which were such monuments of British submis-
sion to rapacity and extortion. He who would see these
houses pining away, let him walk from Basingstoke, or
even Windsor, to London, by way of Hounslow, and mor-
alize on their perishing remains; the stables crumbling to
dust; unsettled labourers and wanderers bivouacking in
the outhouses; grass growing in the yards; the rooms,
where erst so many hundred beds of down were made up,
let off to Irish lodgers at eighteen-pence a week; a little ill-
looking beer-shop shrinking in the tap of former days,
burning coach-house gates for firewood, having one of its
two windows bunged up, as if it had received punishment
in a fight with the Railroad; a low, bandy-legged, brick-
making bull-dog standing in the doorway. What could I
next see in my fire so naturally as the new railway-house of
these times near the dismal country station; with nothing
particular on draught but cold air and damp, nothing
worth mentioning in the larder but new mortar, and no
business doing beyond a conceited affectation of luggage
in the hall? Then I came to the Inns of Paris, with the
pretty apartment of four pieces up one hundred and sev-

enty-five waxed stairs, the privilege of ringing the bell all day long without influencing anybody's mind or body but your own, and the not-too-much-for-dinner, considering the price. Next to the provincial Inns of France, with the great church-tower rising above the courtyard, the horse-bells jingling merrily up and down the street beyond, and the clocks of all descriptions in all the rooms, which are never right, unless taken at the precise minute when, by getting exactly twelve hours too fast or too slow, they unintentionally become so. Away I went, next, to the lesser roadside Inns of Italy; where all the dirty clothes in the house (not in wear) are always lying in your anteroom; where the mosquitoes make a raisin pudding of your face in summer, and the cold bites it blue in winter; where you get what you can, and forget what you can't; where I should again like to be boiling my tea in a pocket-hand-kerchief dumpling, for want of a teapot. So to the old palace Inns and old monastery Inns, in towns and cities of the same bright country; with their massive quadrangular staircases, whence you may look from among clustering pillars high into the blue vault of heaven; with their stately banqueting rooms, and vast refectories; with their labyrinths of ghostly bed-chambers, and their glimpses into gorgeous streets that have no appearance of reality or possibility. So to the close little Inns of the Malaria districts, with their pale attendants, and their peculiar smell of never letting in the air. So to the immense fantastic Inns of Venice, with the cry of the gondolier below, as he skims the corner; the grip of the watery odors on one particular little bit of the bridge of your nose (which is

never released while you stay there); and the great bell of
St. Mark's Cathedral tolling midnight. Next I put up for
a minute at the restless Inns upon the Rhine, where your
going to bed, no matter at what hour, appears to be the
tocsin for everybody else's getting up; and where, in the
table-d'hote room at the end of the long table (with several Towers of Babel on it at the other end, all made of
white plates), one knot of stoutish men, entirely dressed in
jewels and dirt, and having nothing else upon them, *will*
remain all night, clinking glasses, and singing about the
river that flows, and the grape that grows, and Rhine
wine that beguiles, and Rhine woman that smiles and hi
drink drink my friend and ho drink drink my brother, and
all the rest of it. I departed thence, as a matter of course,
to other German Inns, where all the eatables are sodden
down to the same flavor, and where the mind is disturbed
by the apparition of hot puddings, and boiled cherries,
sweet and slab, at awfully unexpected periods of the
repast. After a draught of sparkling beer from a foaming
glass jug, and a glance of recognition through the windows of the student beer-houses at Heidelberg and else-
where, I put out to sea for the Inns of America, with their
four hundred beds apiece, and their eight or nine hundred
ladies and gentlemen at dinner every day. Again I stood in
the bar-rooms, thereof, taking my evening cobbler, julep,
sling, or cocktail. Again I listened to my friend the General,—whom I had known for five minutes, in the course
of which period he had made me intimate for life with two
Majors, who again had made me intimate for life with
three Colonels, who again had made me brother to

twenty-two civilians,—again, I say, I listened to my friend
the General, leisurely expounding the resources of the establishment, as to gentlemen's morning-room, sir; ladies'
morning-room, sir; gentlemen's evening-room, sir; ladies'
evening-room, sir; ladies' and gentlemen's evening re-
uniting-room, sir; music-room, sir; reading-room, sir; over
four hundred sleeping-rooms, sir; and the entire planned
and finited within twelve calendar months from the first
clearing off of the old encumbrances on the plot, at a cost
of five hundred thousand dollars, sir. Again I found, as to
my individual way of thinking, that the greater, the more
gorgeous, and the more dollarous the establishment was,
the less desirable it was. Nevertheless, again I drank my
cobbler, julep, sling, or cocktail, in all good-will, to my
friend the General, and my friends the Majors, Colonels,
and civilians all; full well knowing that, whatever little
motes my beamy eyes may have described in theirs, they
belong to a kind, generous, large-hearted, and great people.

I had been going on lately at a quick pace to keep my
solitude out of my mind; but here I broke down for good,
and gave up the subject. What was I to do? What was to
become of me? Into what extremity was I submissively to
sink? Supposing that, like Baron Trenck, I looked out for
a mouse or spider, and found one, and beguiled my impris-
onment by training it? Even that might be dangerous with
a view to the future. I might be so far gone when the road
did come to be cut through the snow, that, on my way
forth, I might burst into tears, and beseech, like the prisoner who was released in his old age from the Bastille, to

be taken back again to the five windows, the ten curtains, and the sinuous drapery.

A desperate idea came into my head. Under any other circumstances I should have rejected it; but, in the strait at which I was, I held it fast. Could I so far overcome the inherent bashfulness which withheld me from the landlord's table and the company I might find there, as to call up the Boots, and ask him to take a chair,—and something in a liquid form,—and talk to me? I could. I would. I did.

SECOND BRANCH
The Boots

Where had he been in his time? he repeated, when I asked him the question. Lord, he had been everywhere! And what had he been? Bless you, he had been everything you could mention a'most!

Seen a good deal? Why, of course he had. I should say so, he could assure me, if I only knew about a twentieth part of what had come in *his* way. Why, it would be easier for him, he expected, to tell what he hadn't seen than what he had. Ah! A deal, it would.

What was the curiousest thing he had seen? Well! He didn't know. He couldn't momently name what was the curiousest thing he had seen,—unless it was a Unicorn,— and he see *him* once at a Fair. But supposing a young gentleman not eight year old was to run away with a fine young woman of seven, might I think *that* a queer start? Certainly. Then that was a start as he himself had had his blessed eyes on, and he had cleaned the shoes they run away in—and they was so little that he couldn't get his hand into 'em.

Master Harry Walmers' father, you see, he lived at the Elmses, down away by Shooter's Hill there, six or seven miles from Lunnon. He was a gentleman of spirit, and good-looking, and held his head up when he walked, and had what you may call Fire about him. He wrote poetry, and he rode, and he ran, and he cricketed, and he danced, and he acted, and he done it all equally beautiful. He was uncommon proud of Master Harry as was his only child; but he didn't spoil him neither. He was a gentleman that had a will of his own and a eye of his own, and that would be minded. Consequently, though he made quite a companion of the fine bright boy, and was delighted to see him so fond of reading his fairy books, and was never tired of hearing him say my name is Norval, or hearing him sing his songs about Young May Moons is beaming love, and When he as adores thee has left but the name, and that; still he kept the command over the child, and the child *was* a child, and it's to be wished more of 'em was!

How did Boots happen to know all this? Why, through being under-gardener. Of course he couldn't be under-gardener, and be always about, in the summer-time, near the windows on the lawn, a mowing, and sweeping, and weeding, and pruning, and this and that, without getting acquainted with the ways of the family. Even supposing Master Harry hadn't come to him one morning early, and said, "Cobbs, how should you spell Norah, if you was asked?" and then began cutting it in print all over the fence.

He couldn't say he had taken particular notice of children before that; but really it was pretty to see them two mites a going about the place together, deep in love. And the courage of the boy! Bless your soul, he'd have throwed off his little hat, and tucked up his little sleeves, and gone in at a Lion, he would, if they had happened to meet one, and she had been frightened of him. One day he stops, along with her, where Boots was hoeing weeds in the gravel, and says, speaking up, "Cobbs," he says, "I like *you.*" "Do you, sir? I'm proud to hear it." "Yes, I do, Cobbs. Why do I like you, do you think, Cobbs?" "Don't know, Master Harry, I am sure." "Because Norah likes you, Cobbs." "Indeed, sir? That's very gratifying." "Gratifying, Cobbs? It's better than millions of the brightest diamonds to be liked by Norah." "Certainly, sir." "You're going away, ain't you, Cobbs?" "Yes, sir." "Would you like another situation, Cobbs?" "Well, sir, I shouldn't object, if it was a good 'un." "Then, Cobbs," says he, "you shall be our Head Gardener when we are married." And he tucks her, in her little sky-blue mantle, under his arm, and walks away.

Boots could assure me that it was better than a picter, and equal to a play, to see them babies, with their long, bright, curling hair, their sparkling eyes, and their beautiful light tread, a rambling about the garden, deep in love. Boots was of opinion that the birds believed they was birds, and kept up with 'em, singing to please 'em. Sometimes they would creep under the Tulip-tree, and would

sit there with their arms round one another's necks, and
their soft cheeks touching, a reading about the Prince and
the Dragon, and the good and bad enchanters, and the
king's fair daughter. Sometimes he would hear them planning about having a house in a forest, keeping bees and a
cow, and living entirely on milk and honey. Once he came
upon them by the pond, and heard Master Harry say,
"Adorable Norah, kiss me, and say you love me to distraction, or I'll jump in head-foremost." And Boots made
no question he would have done it if she hadn't complied.
On the whole, Boots said it had a tendency to make him
feel as if he was in love himself—only he didn't exactly
know who with.

"Cobbs," said Master Harry, one evening, when Cobbs
was watering the flowers, "I am going on a visit, this
present Midsummer, to my grandmamma's at York."

"Are you indeed, sir? I hope you'll have a pleasant
time. I am going into Yorkshire myself, when I leave
here."

"Are you going to your grandmamma's, Cobbs?"

"No, sir. I haven't got such a thing."

"Not as a grandmamma, Cobbs?"

"No, sir."

The boy looked on at the watering of the flowers for a
little while, and then said, "I shall be very glad indeed to
go, Cobbs,—Norah's going."

"You'll be all right then, sir," says Cobb, "with your
beautiful sweetheart by your side."

"Cobbs," returned the boy, flushing, "I never let anybody joke about it, when I can prevent them."

"It wasn't a joke, sir," says Cobbs, with humility,— "wasn't so meant."

"I am glad of that, Cobbs, because I like you, you know, and you're going to live with us.—Cobbs!"

"Sir."

"What do you think my grandmamma gives me when I go down there?"

"I couldn't so much as make a guess, sir."

"A Bank of England five-pound note, Cobbs."

"Whew!" says Cobbs, "that's a spanking sum of money, Master Harry."

"A person could do a good deal with such a sum of money as that,—couldn't a person, Cobbs?"

"I believe you, sir!"

"Cobbs," said the boy, "I'll tell you a secret. At Norah's house, they have been joking her about me, and pretending to laugh at our being engaged,—pretending to make game of it, Cobbs!"

"Such, sir," says Cobbs, "is the depravity of human natur."

The boy, looking exactly like his father, stood for a few minutes with his glowing face towards the sunset, and then departed with, "Good-night, Cobbs. I'm going in."

If I was to ask Boots how it happened that he was a going to leave that place just at that present time, well, he couldn't rightly answer me. He did suppose he might have stayed there till now if he had been anyways inclined. But, you see, he was younger then, and he wanted change. That's what he wanted,—change. Mr. Walmers, he said to him when he gave him notice of his intentions to leave,

"Cobbs," he says, "have you anything to complain of? I make the inquiry because if I find that any of my people really has anything to complain of, I wish to make it right if I can." "No, sir," says Cobbs; "thanking you, sir, I find myself as well sitiwated here as I could hope to be anywheres. The truth is, sir, that I'm a going to seek my fortun'." "O, indeed, Cobbs!" he says; "I hope you may find it." And Boots could assure me—which he did, touching his hair with his bootjack, as a salute in the way of his present calling—that he hadn't found it yet.

Well, sir! Boots left the Elmses when his time was up, and Master Harry, he went down to the old lady's at York, which old lady would have given that child the teeth out of her head (if she had had any), she was so wrapped up in him. What does that Infant do,—for Infant you may call him and be within the mark,—but cut away from that old lady's with his Norah, on a expedition to go to Gretna Green and be married!

Sir, Boots was at this identical Holly-Tree Inn (having left it several times since to better himself, but always come back through one thing or another), when, one summer afternoon, the coach drives up, and out of the coach gets them two children. The Guard says to our Governor, "I don't quite make out these little passengers, but the young gentleman's words was, that they was to be brought here." The young gentleman gets out; hands his lady out; gives the Guard something for himself; says to our Governor, "We're to stop here tonight, please. Sitting-room and two bed-rooms will be required. Chops and cherry-pudding for two!" and tucks her, in her little sky-blue mantle, under his arm, and walks into the house much bolder than Brass.

Boots leaves me to judge what the amazement of that establishment was, when these two tiny creatures all alone by themselves was marched into the Angel,—much more so, when he, who had seen them without their seeing him, give the Governor his views of the expedition they was upon. "Cobbs," says the Governor, "if this is so, I must set off myself to York, and quiet their friends' minds. In which case you must keep your eye upon 'em, and humor 'em, till I come back. But before I take these measures, Cobbs, I should wish you to find from themselves whether your opinion is correct." "Sir, to you," says Cobbs, "that shall be done directly."

So Boots goes upstairs to the Angel, and there he finds Master Harry on a enormous sofa,—immense at any time, but looking like the Great Bed of Ware, compared with him,—a drying the eyes of Miss Norah with his pocket-handkecher. Their little legs was entirely off the ground, of course, and it really is not possible for Boots to express to me how small them children looked.

"It's Cobbs! It's Cobbs!" cried Master Harry, and comes running to him, and catching hold of his hand. Miss Norah comes running to him on t' other side and catching hold of his t' other hand, and they both jump for joy.

"I see you a getting out, sir," says Cobbs. "I thought it was you. I thought I couldn't be mistaken in your height and figure. What's the object of your journey, sir?—Matrimonial?"

"We are going to be married, Cobbs, at Gretna Green," returned the boy. "We have run away on purpose. Norah has been in rather low spirits, Cobbs; but she'll be happy, now we have found you to be our friend."

"Thank you, sir, and thank *you*, miss," says Cobbs, for your good opinion. *Did* you bring any luggage with you, sir?"

If I will believe Boots when he gives me his word and honor upon it, the lady had got a parasol, a smelling-bottle, a round and a half of cold buttered toast, eight peppermint drops, and a hair-brush,—seemingly a doll's. The gentleman had got about half a dozen yards of string, a knife, three or four sheets of writing-paper folded up surprisingly small, a orange, and a Chaney mug with his name upon it.

"What may be the exact nature of your plans, sir?" says Cobbs.

"To go on," replied the boy,—which the courage of that boy was something wonderful!—"in the morning, and be married tomorrow."

"Just so, sir," says Cobbs. "Would it meet your views, sir, if I was to accompany you?"

When Cobbs said this, they both jumped for joy again, and cried out, "Oh, yes, yes, Cobbs! Yes!"

"Well, sir," says Cobbs. "If you will excuse my having the freedom to give an opinion, what I should recommend would be this. I'm acquainted with a pony, sir, which, put in a pheayton that I could borrow, would take you and Mrs. Harry Walmers, Junior (myself driving, if you approved,) to the end of your journey in a very short space of time. I am not altogether sure, sir, that this pony will be at liberty tomorrow, but even if you had to wait over tomorrow for him, it might be worth your while. As to the small account here, sir, in case you was to find yourself running at all short, that don't signify; because I'm a part proprietor of this inn, and it could stand over."

Boots assures me that when they clapped their hands, and jumped for joy again, and called him "Good Cobbs!" and "Dear Cobbs!" and bent across him to kiss one another in the delight of their confiding hearts, he felt himself the meanest rascal for deceiving 'em that ever was born.

"Is there anything you want just at present, sir?" says Cobbs, mortally ashamed of himself.

"We should like some cakes after dinner," answered Master Harry, folding his arms, putting out one leg, and looking straight at him, "and two apples,—and jam. With dinner we should like to have toast-and-water. But Norah has always been accustomed to half a glass of currant wine at dessert. And so have I."

"It shall be ordered at the bar, sir," says Cobbs; and away he went.

Boots has the feeling as fresh upon him at this minute of speaking as he had then, that he would far rather have had it out in half a dozen rounds with the Governor than have combined with him; and that he wished with all his heart there was any impossible place where those two babies could make an impossible marriage, and live impossibly happy ever afterwards. However, as it couldn't be, he went into the Governor's plans, and the Governor set off for York in half an hour.

The way in which the women of that house—without exception—every one of 'em—married *and* single—took to that boy when they heard the story, Boots considers surprising. It was as much as he could do to keep 'em from dashing into the room and kissing him. They climbed up all sorts of places, at the risk of their lives, to look at him through a pane of glass. They was seven deep at the keyhole. They was out of their minds about him and his bold spirit.

In the evening, Boots went into the room to see how the runaway couple was getting on. The gentleman was on the windowseat, supporting the lady in his arms. She had tears upon her face, and was lying, very tired and half asleep, with her head upon his shoulder.

"Mrs. Harry Walmers, Junior, fatigued, sir?" says Cobbs.

"Yes, she is tired, Cobbs; but she is not used to be away from home, and she has been in low spirits again. Cobbs, do you think you could bring a biffin, please?"

"I ask your pardon, sir," says Cobbs. "What was it you—?"

"I think a Norfolk biffin would rouse her, Cobbs. She is very fond of them."

Boots withdrew in search of the required restorative, and, when he brought it in, the gentleman handed it to the lady, and fed her with a spoon, and took a little himself; the lady being heavy with sleep, and rather cross. "What should you think, sir," says Cobbs, "of a chamber candle-stick?" The gentleman approved; the chambermaid went first, up the great staircase; the lady, in her sky-blue mantle, followed, gallantly escorted by the gentleman; the gentleman embraced her at her door, and retired to his own apartment, where Boots softly locked him up.

Boots couldn't but feel with increased acuteness what a base deceiver he was, when they consulted him at breakfast (they had ordered sweet milk-and-water and toast and currant jelly, overnight) about the pony. It really was as much as he could do, he don't mind confessing to me, to look them two young things in the face, and think what a wicked old father of lies he had grown up to be. Howsomever, he went on a lying like a Trojan about the pony. He told 'em that it did so unfort'nately happen that the pony was half clipped, you see, and that he couldn't be taken out in that state, for fear it should strike to his inside. But that he'd be finished clipping in the course of the day, and that tomorrow morning at eight o'clock the pheayton would be ready. Boots's view of the whole case, looking back on it in my room, is, that Mrs. Harry Walmers, Junior, was beginning to give in. She hadn't had her hair curled when she went to bed, and she didn't seem quite up to brushing it herself, and its getting in her eyes put her out. But nothing put out Master Harry. He sat behind his breakfast-cup, a tearing away at the jelly, as if he had been his own father.

After breakfast, Boots is inclined to consider that they drawed soldiers,—at least, he knows that many such was found in the fireplace, all on horseback. In the course of the morning, Master Harry rang the bell,—it was surprising how that there boy did carry on,—and said, in a sprightly way, "Cobbs, is there any good walks in this neighborhood?"

"Yes, sir," says Cobbs. "There's Love Lane."

"Get out with you, Cobbs!"—that was that there boy's expression,—"you're joking."

"Begging your pardon, sir," says Cobb, "there really is Love Lane. And a pleasant walk it is, and proud shall I be to show it to yourself and Mrs. Harry Walmers, Junior."

"Norah, dear," said Master Harry, "this is curious. We really ought to see Love Lane. Put on your bonnet, my sweetest darling, and we will go there with Cobbs."

Boots leaves me to judge what a Beast he felt himself to be, when that young pair told him, as they all three jogged along together, that they had made up their minds to give him two thousand guineas a year as head-gardener, on accounts of his being so true a friend to 'em. Boots could have wished at the moment that the earth would have opened and swallowed him up, he felt so mean, with their beaming eyes a looking at him, and believing him. Well, sir, he turned the conversation as well as he could, and he took 'em down Love Lane to the water-meadows, and there Master Harry would have drowned himself in half a moment more, a getting out a water-lily for her,—but nothing daunted that boy. Well, sir, they was tired out. All being so new and strange to 'em, they was tired as tired could be. And they laid down on a bank of daisies, like the children in the wood, leastways meadows, and fell asleep.

Boots don't know—perhaps I do,—but never mind, it

don't signify either way—why it made a man fit to make a fool of himself to see them two pretty babies a lying there in the clear, still, sunny day, not dreaming half so hard when they was asleep as they done when they was awake. But, Lord! when you come to think of yourself, you know, and what a game you have been up to ever since you was in your own cradle, and what a poor sort of a chap you are, and how it's always either Yesterday with you, or else Tomorrow, and never Today, that's where it is!

Well, sir, they woke up at last, and then one thing was getting pretty clear to Boots, namely, that Mrs. Harry Walmerses, Junior's, temper was on the move. When Master Harry took her round the waist, she said he "teased her so;" and when he says, "Norah, my young May Moon, your Harry tease you?" she tells him, "Yes; and I want to go home!"

A biled fowl, and baked bread-and-butter pudding, brought Mrs. Walmers up a little; but Boots could have wished, he must privately own to me, to have seen her more sensible of the voice of love, and less abandoning of herself to currants. However, Master Harry, he kept up, and his noble heart was as fond as ever. Mrs. Walmers turned very sleepy about dusk, and began to cry. Therefore, Mrs. Walmers went off to bed as per yesterday; and Master Harry ditto repeated.

About eleven or twelve at night comes back the Governor in a chaise, along with Mr. Walmers and a elderly lady. Mr. Walmers looks amused and very serious, both at once, and says to our missis, "We are much indebted to you, ma'am, for your kind care of our little children, which we can never sufficiently acknowledge. Pray, ma'am, where is my boy?" Our missis, says, "Cobbs has the dear child in charge, sir. Cobbs, show Forty!" Then he says to Cobbs, "Ah, Cobbs, I am glad to see *you!* I understood you was here!" And Cobbs says, "Yes, sir. Your most obedient, sir."

I may be surprised to hear Boots say it, perhaps; but Boots assures me that his heart beat like a hammer, going upstairs. "I beg your pardon, sir," says he, while unlocking the door; "I hope you are not angry with Master Harry. For Master Harry is a fine boy, sir, and will do you credit and honor." And Boots signifies to me, that, if the fine boy's father had contradicted him in the daring state of mind in which he then was, he thinks he should have "fetched him a crack," and taken the consequences.

But Mr. Walmers only says, "No, Cobbs. No, my good fellow. Thank you!" And, the door being opened, goes in.

Boots goes in too, holding the light, and he sees Mr. Walmers go up to the bedside, bend gently down, and kiss the little sleeping face. Then he stands looking at it for a minute, looking wonderfully like it (they do say he ran away with Mrs. Walmers); and then he gently shakes the little shoulder.

"Harry, my dear boy! Harry!"

Master Harry starts up and looks at him. Looks at Cobbs too. Such is the honor of that mite, that he looks at Cobbs, to see whether he has brought him into trouble.

"I am not angry, my child. I only want you to dress yourself and come home."

"Yes, pa."

Master Harry dresses himself quickly. His breast begins to swell when he has nearly finished, and it swells more and more as he stands, at last, a looking at his father: his father standing a looking at him, the quiet image of him.

"Please may I"—the spirit of that little creature, and the way he kept his rising tears down!—"please, dear pa—may I—kiss Norah before I go?"

"You may, my child."

So he takes Master Harry in his hand, and Boots leads the way with the candle, and they come to that other bedroom, where the elderly lady is seated by the bed, and poor little Mrs. Harry Walmers, Junior, is fast asleep. There the father lifts the child up to the pillow, and he lays his little face down for an instant by the little warm face of poor unconscious little Mrs. Harry Walmers, Junior, and gently draws it to him,—a sight so touching to the chambermaids who are peeping through the door, that one of them calls out, "It's a shame to part 'em!" But this chambermaid was always, as Boots informs me, a soft-hearted one. Not that there was any harm in that girl. Far from it.

Finally, Boots says, that's all about it. Mr. Walmers drove away in the chaise, having hold of Master Harry's hand. The elderly lady and Mrs. Harry Walmers, Junior, that was never to be (she married a Captain long afterwards, and died in India), went off next day. In conclusion, Boots put it to me whether I hold with him in two opinions: firstly, that there are not many couples on their way to be married who are half as innocent of guile as those two children; secondly, that it would be a jolly good thing for a great many couples on their way to be married, if they could only be stopped in time, and brought back separately.

THIRD BRANCH
The Bill

I had been snowed up a whole week. The time had hung so lightly on my hands, that I should have been in great doubt of the fact but for a piece of documentary evidence that lay upon my table.

The road had been dug out of the snow on the previous day, and the document in question was my bill. It testified emphatically to my having eaten and drunk, and warmed myself, and slept among the sheltering branches of the Holly-Tree, seven days and nights.

I had yesterday allowed the road twenty-four hours to improve itself, finding that I required that additional margin of time for the completion of my task. I had ordered my Bill to be upon the table, and a chaise to be at the door, "at eight o'clock tomorrow evening." It was eight o'clock tomorrow evening when I buckled up my traveling writing-desk in its leather case, paid my Bill, and got on my warm coats and wrappers. Of course, no time now remained for my traveling on to add a frozen tear to the icicles which were doubtless hanging plentifully about the farmhouse where I had first seen Angela. What I had to do was to get across to Liverpool by the shortest open road, there to meet my heavy baggage and embark. It was quite enough to do, and I had not an hour too much time to do it in.

I had taken leave of all my Holly-Tree friends—almost, for the time being, of my bashfulness too—and was standing for half a minute at the Inn door watching the ostler as he took another turn at the cord which tied my portmanteau on the chaise, when I saw lamps coming down towards the Holly-Tree. The road was so padded with snow that no wheels were audible; but all of us who were standing at the Inn door saw lamps coming on, and at a lively rate too, between the walls of snow that had been heaped up on either side of the track. The chambermaid instantly divined how the case stood, and called to the ostler, "Tom, this is a Gretna job!" The ostler, knowing that her sex instinctively scented a marriage, or anything in that direction, rushed up the yard bawling, "Next four out!" and in a moment the whole establishment was thrown into commotion.

I had a melancholy interest in seeing the happy man who loved and was beloved; and therefore, instead of driving off at once, I remained at the Inn door when the fugitives drove up. A bright-eyed fellow, muffled in a mantle, jumped out so briskly that he almost overthrew me. He turned to apologize, and, by Heaven, it was Edwin!

"Charley!" said he, recoiling. "Gracious powers, what do you do here?"

"Edwin," said I, recoiling, "gracious powers, what do *you* do here?" I struck my forehead as I said it, and an insupportable blaze of light seemed to shoot before my eyes.

He hurried me into the little parlor (always kept with a slow fire in it and no poker), where posting company waited while their horses were putting to, and, shutting the door, said:

"Charley, forgive me!"

"Edwin!" I returned. "Was this well? When I loved her so dearly! When I had garnered up my heart so long!" I could say no more.

He was shocked when he saw how moved I was, and made the cruel observation, that he had not thought I should have taken it so much to heart.

I looked at him. I reproached him no more. But I looked at him.

"My dear, dear Charley," said he, "don't think ill of me, I beseech you! I know you have a right to my utmost confidence, and, believe me, you have ever had it until now. I abhor secrecy. Its meanness is intolerable to me. But I and my dear girl have observed it for your sake."

He and his dear girl! It steeled me.

"You have observed it for my sake, sir?" said I, wondering how his frank face could face it out so.

"Yes!—and Angela's," said he.

I found the room reeling round in an uncertain way, like a laboring humming-top. "Explain yourself," said I, holding on by one hand to an arm-chair.

"Dear old darling Charley!" returned Edwin, in his cordial manner, "consider! When you were going on so happily with Angela, why should I compromise you with the old gentleman by making you a party to our engagement, and (after he had declined my proposals) to our secret intention? Surely it was better that you should be able honorably to say, 'He never took counsel with me, never told me, never breathed a word of it.' If Angela suspected it, and showed me all the favor and support she could—God bless her for a precious creature and a priceless wife—I couldn't help that. Neither I nor Emmeline ever told her, any more than we told you. And for the same good reason, Charley; trust me, for the same good reason, and no other upon earth!"

Emmeline was Angela's cousin. Lived with her. Had been brought up with her. Was her father's ward. Had property.

"Emmeline is in the chaise, my dear Edwin!" said I, embracing him with the greatest affection.

"My good fellow!" said he, "do you suppose I should be going to Gretna Green without her?"

I ran out with Edwin, I opened the chaise door, I took Emmeline in my arms, I folded her to my heart. She was wrapped in soft white fur, like the snowy landscape: but was warm, and young, and lovely. I put their leaders to with my own hands, I gave the boys a five-pound note apiece, I cheered them as they drove away, I drove the other way myself as hard as I could pelt.

I never went to Liverpool, I never went to America, I went straight back to London, and I married Angela. I have never until this time, even to her, disclosed the secret of my character, and the mistrust and the mistaken journey into which it led me. When she, and they, and our eight children and their seven—I mean Edwin's and Emmeline's, whose eldest girl is old enough now to wear white for herself, and to look very like her mother in it—come to read these pages, as of course they will, I shall hardly fail to be found out at last. Never mind! I can bear it. I began at the Holly-Tree, by idle accident, to associate the Christmastime of year with human interest, and with some inquiry into, and some care for, the lives of those by whom I find myself surrounded. I hope that I am none the worse for it, and that no one near me or afar off is the worse for it. And I say, May the green Holly-Tree flourish, striking its roots deep into our English ground, and having its germinating qualities carried by the birds of Heaven all over the world!